blood wounds

blood wounds

[Susan Beth Pfeffer]

Houghton Mifflin Harcourt

Boston   New York

www.hmhbooks.com

The text of this book is set in Garamond Pro.

The Library of Congress has cataloged the hardcover edition as follows:
Pfeffer, Susan Beth, 1948–.
Blood wounds / Susan Beth Pfeffer.
p. cm.
Summary: Willa seems to have a perfect life as a member of a loving blended
family until the estranged father she barely remembers murders his wife and
children, then heads toward Willa and her mother.
[1. Murder—Fiction. 2. Family life—Pennsylvania—Fiction. 3. Stepfami-
lies—Fiction. 4. Cutting (Self-mutilation)—Fiction. 5. Self-mutilation—Fiction. 6. Secrets—Fiction.] I. Title.
PZ7.P44855Blo 2011
[Fic]—dc22
2011009602

ISBN: 978-0-547-49638-2 hardcover
ISBN: 978-0-547-85506-6 paperback

Manufactured in the United States of America
DOC 10 9 8 7 6 5 4 3 2 1

4500371808

To
Felipe, Margarita, Philippe, and Victoria

part one
[happy families]

one

I THINK EVEN IF NOTHING had happened the next day, even if my life had stayed just as it was that night at supper, I'd still remember what Jack said. He has that way of startling me by saying something totally unexpected but then, when I think about it, something that makes perfect sense, something I should have known all along.

We were all at the supper table. It was Wednesday night, and Wednesday nights we eat together. Jack has Tuesdays and Wednesdays off, but we could never manage two nights in a row. Mom's committed to completing her bachelor's degree, so she takes a couple of classes during the day and one or two at night. Brooke always has something: lacrosse, dressage, violin, not to mention her dozens of friends. Alyssa has tennis plus the swimming and yoga she uses for cross-training. And I keep busy enough too, with choir and the occasional school play.

But Wednesday nights we eat together. Jack does the shopping and the cooking, and whoever is around pitches in to help. This time Alyssa made the salad and Brooke set the table. I had a choir rehearsal and got home only a few minutes before suppertime.

I wouldn't remember any of that if everything hadn't changed the next day. But I'm sure I would remember what Jack said.

Mom was telling us about her nineteenth-century literature class. Mom wants to be a fourth-grade teacher, and fourth-grade teachers don't need to know much about nineteenth-century literature, but it's always bothered her that Jack's so well read and she isn't. And Val, Brooke and Alyssa's mother, who lives in Orlando, sends them lots of books, current bestsellers mostly, but sometimes a classic she thinks they should read.

"Have you decided what you're going to do your paper on, Terri?" Brooke asked Mom.

Mom took a bite of the tilapia and shook her head. "I'd like to do it on *Jane Eyre*," she said. "But my professor said she's read too many papers on *Jane Eyre* and we have to pick something else. She said not enough students write papers on *War and Peace,* but I'm not even sure I'll finish it before the final. *War and Peace* is awfully long."

"I don't like long books," Alyssa said. "I think there should be a rule that books can't be more than two hundred pages."

"There'd be a lot fewer good books with that rule," Brooke said.

"Yeah," I said. "But there'd be a lot more trees."

"You know something?" Jack said, as we sat at the table, eating and laughing. "Tolstoy was wrong."

"About what?" Brooke asked, helping herself to the string beans.

"Who's Tolstoy?" Alyssa asked.

"He wrote *War and Peace,*" Mom said. "And a lot of other very long books. What was Tolstoy wrong about, darling?"

"He said all happy families are alike," Jack replied. "Unhappy families are all different."

"What's wrong about that?" I asked.

"Well, look at us," Jack said. "We're a happy family. But we're not identical to other happy families. Happy families come in their own shapes and varieties, same as the unhappy ones."

"Are we going to stay a happy family if I go to USC?" Brooke asked.

"I thought you were going to go to North Carolina," I said, "and take that lacrosse scholarship."

"I haven't decided yet," Brooke said. "So, Dad, how happy will we be if I pick USC instead?"

"North Carolina's kind of equidistant between us and Orlando," I said. "If you go to USC, we'll hardly ever see you."

"Brooke said she hasn't decided yet," Mom said to me.

"I know," I said. "I heard her."

Jack looked straight at Brooke. "Have you talked to your mother about it?" he asked.

"Not yet," Brooke said. "We've both been too busy to talk."

"Speaking of your mother, she called today," Jack said. "There are some changes in plans for your spring vacation."

"What changes?" Alyssa asked. "She's taking me to Brussels, right? For the tournament?"

"Dad, it was all set," Brooke said. "Terri and I were meeting Mom in Maryland for my dressage test. Then she was coming back here to take Lyss to Brussels. What happened this time?"

"First of all, I would appreciate it if you didn't use that tone of voice when you're talking about your mother," Jack said.

"I'm sorry, Dad," Brooke said. "But I know I'm not going to like what's coming."

"No, it isn't that bad," Jack said. "Your mother's trip to Munich was postponed, so she won't be able to come here."

"But I can still go to Brussels," Alyssa said, and I could hear the panic in her voice. "Daddy, it's my first international tournament. I've got to go."

"Your mother understands that," Jack said. "So she asked her parents to fly here. Gram will go with you and Terri to the dressage test, Brooke, and Grandy will take Alyssa to Brussels." He smiled at his daughters. "Monday, Gram and Brooke will fly to Switzerland for a few days of skiing, then go on to Brussels, and you'll all fly back together."

"Mom was going to see me play," Alyssa said. "I want her to see how good I've gotten."

"She wants to see it too," Jack said. "She's hoping to get to Brussels for the quarterfinals."

None of us asked what would happen if Alyssa didn't make it to the quarters. She always did.

"Lauren's in Europe, isn't she?" Alyssa asked me.

Lauren is my best friend, my only real friend outside of the kids in choir. She's spending her junior year abroad.

"Spain," I said. "Madrid."

"I was looking forward to being home for the week," Brooke said. "Have a do-nothing vacation, like Willa."

"Willa's going to keep busy enough," Mom said. "She'll be working on turning her B's into A's."

"Willa's grades are fine," Jack said. He smiled at me. "Maybe we'll take an overnight trip to Washington," he said. "Go to the Smithsonian. Tour the White House. What do you say, Terri? Think we could swing that?"

Mom nodded. "That sounds nice," she said.

"Good," Jack said. "It's settled. Brooke and Alyssa with their mom and grandparents. You and Willa and me with the president."

Once, when I was eleven, before we moved so Brooke and Alyssa could live with us, Jack found me sitting on the kitchen floor, crying. He asked me what was the matter, and I told him that all the girls in sixth grade were prettier than me.

"Oh, pumpkin," Jack said. "You don't want to waste your pretty years in middle school. Not on middle-school boys. Wait until they're ready to see how beautiful you are. High school, or even college. You can hold off until then, can't you?"

"Will I really be pretty then?" I asked him.

Jack helped me up off the floor and hugged me. "You'll be as pretty as you want to be," he said. "And all the boys will notice."

I'm sixteen now, and a long way from beautiful, but I've noticed that on days when I feel pretty, the boys in my school do seem to notice. And I'm glad I didn't waste my pretty years on middle school.

That night, at supper, I knew we really were a happy family. Happy didn't mean all singing and dancing. Brooke and Alyssa weren't shy about letting Mom or Jack know when they were unhappy about something. There were battles of will, flashes of temper.

But I knew enough about stepfathers and stepsisters to understand how lucky we were, how hard Jack and Mom worked to make sure we knew we were part of the same family, equally loved by both of them.

It couldn't have been easy for either of them. Jack already shared custody with Val when Mom met him. The first few years after they got married, the three of us lived in a house about an hour away from Val's. Brooke and Alyssa spent practically every weekend with us, and Christmas vacation, and summer when they weren't at camp or visiting their grandparents. Jack was a sports reporter for the *Union Gazette*, so he worked on weekends, but that didn't matter. Brooke was busy with dressage, and Alyssa with tennis lessons, so Mom did the chauffeuring, and either I'd tag along with her or I'd go to football or basketball games with Jack. I liked it best when Brooke came with us. She's a year older than I am, and I worshiped her. Alyssa is two years younger than I am, but she only worships other tennis players.

We were a happy family then too. We even stayed a happy

family when Val got transferred for three years to Shanghai. Alyssa refused to go with her, and Brooke admitted she didn't want to.

Jack and Mom had a lot of discussions about the situation, none of which I was supposed to hear but did anyway. Val came over a few times when Alyssa was at tennis practice and Brooke was taking her violin lesson. I made sure to eavesdrop then.

But even with all my spying, I was still shocked when Jack and Mom and Val sat us down together and explained what was going to happen. Jack and Mom were going to sell our house and buy one in Westbridge, where Brooke and Alyssa lived. That way they could continue to go to Fairhaven Academy, and Alyssa could keep her tennis coach and Brooke her violin teacher and riding academy. Mom would quit her job so that she'd be available to take Brooke and Alyssa where they needed to go (Val's housekeeper used to do that). Jack's commute would be a little longer, and I'd transfer to the middle school in Westbridge. It was easier for us to move than for Brooke's and Alyssa's lives to be disrupted.

I'd grown up with Brooke and Alyssa, and they were as close as sisters to me, but that didn't keep me from crying that night. Mom came into my room, sat on my bed, and held my hand.

"I know this isn't easy for you, Willa," she said. "But it

would break Jack's heart if Brooke and Alyssa went with Val to Shanghai."

"But why can't they move here?" I cried. "Why do we have to give up everything?"

"We're not giving up everything," Mom said. "We're moving from one nice house to another one, and you're changing schools. I'll get to be a stay-at-home mom, for you and Brooke and Alyssa. Think of what the girls are giving up. They'll only get to see Val once or twice a year for the next three years. You'll still have Jack and me and our home together."

"But I don't want to start a new school in February," I said. "It's not fair."

Mom kissed me on my cheek. "Shush," she said. "You don't want Jack to hear you, honey. He has to do what's best for the girls. It'll be fine. You'll see."

I wanted to ask Mom if Jack would still love me, but even though I knew her answer would be yes, of course he would, I was too frightened to ask. Instead I did everything I could to make the move easier, and even when we all settled in together and Mom told us that Brooke would have her own room, since she was the oldest, and Alyssa and I would share, I didn't complain. Alyssa did, loud and long, but she didn't have to worry about losing Jack and she didn't seem to care if she lost Mom.

But Jack and Mom made it work. Jack flew with Brooke and Alyssa to Shanghai every Christmas, and Val stopped by each summer and took her daughters on vacation trips to London and Paris and Rome. Brooke left Fairhaven Academy for Westbridge High and added lacrosse to her activities. Alyssa stayed on at Fairhaven, continued with her tennis, and was ranked sixteenth nationally in her age group.

Because Jack had never adopted me, my name hadn't been changed to McDougal. Everyone at school knew Brooke McDougal, but only those kids who knew her or me well knew we were stepsisters. To everyone else, I was just Willa Coffey, reasonably pretty, with a nice voice, good grades, and a handful of friends.

two

I REMEMBER SOMETHING ELSE that happened that night, something I might not have remembered if things had stayed the same.

It was after supper. Alyssa and I were in our room. I was studying for my French test. Alyssa, who should have been studying, was on her laptop. Brooke knocked on the door and came in carrying three red sweaters. Two were bright red and one was burgundy, but they were all red sweaters.

"Mom's been going crazy since she came back," Brooke said. "I didn't even know they sold sweaters in Orlando."

Val had been transferred to Orlando in August. Brooke

didn't want to start a new high school senior year, and although Alyssa had been willing to move to Florida, it was only to go to a tennis academy and Jack had said she was too young. Val had taken to sending the girls packages two or three times a week, clothes mostly, but also books and jewelry and whatever was newest in electronics.

"What are you going to do with all those sweaters?" Alyssa asked.

"There's no point keeping them," Brooke said. "There're another three in my bedroom. Willa, would you like a red sweater? Or two? Or five?"

This was a ritual we had. Brooke always asked me first if I wanted what she was discarding. And I always said no, since I was uncomfortable taking things that her mother had paid for.

"How about you, Lyss?" Brooke asked. "Could I interest you in a red sweater or two? Or five?"

"No, thanks," Alyssa said. "Mom's sent me a half dozen too."

"I'll give mine to the St. James rummage sale, then," Brooke said. "Someone might as well get use out of them."

The St. James rummage sale has made a fortune from Brooke's donations over the years. I've bought a few things there myself, but never anything Brooke donated.

"Do you really think you'll go to USC?" I asked.

"If I can convince Mom," Brooke replied. "She's the one who'll be paying."

"Would you take Sweetbriar with you?" Alyssa asked.

"She's not worth transporting," Brooke said. "I've wanted a better horse for a while now anyway. Someone will buy her."

Val had given Brooke Sweetbriar for her ninth birthday. I still remembered how astounded I'd been that someone could actually own a horse.

Brooke looked thoughtful. "Maybe this vacation thing will work out," she said. "If Gram sees me on Sweetbriar, she'll see why I need a new horse. And if I'm at USC, she and Grandy can come over from Palm Springs to see me ride. I'll ask them for a horse for my birthday, and Mom can give me a car, and Daddy won't be able to say a thing."

Brooke had been complaining since she got her license that all her friends had cars and she didn't. But this was the first time I'd heard her say she wanted a new horse. "I'll miss Sweetbriar," I said.

"That's because you don't have to ride her," Brooke said. "Okay, it's set. Dressage in Maryland, a nice long flight to talk about horses, then a few days of skiing."

"How about coming with us, Willa?" Alyssa asked.

"With you where?" I asked.

"To Brussels," Alyssa said. "I've been looking it up and

there are plenty of flights from Brussels to Madrid. You could fly with us and visit Lauren and then come back and see me in the quarterfinals. You have a passport, don't you?"

I did. Mom had gotten me one a few years ago, just so I'd have one like Brooke and Alyssa. Only they used theirs.

"I can't afford a trip to Europe," I said, which was something Alyssa knew perfectly well.

"Gram and Grandy would pay if we asked them," Alyssa said. "They like you, Willa. They're always telling me you're a good influence, because you're so quiet and well behaved. You'd only have to pay for roundtrip between Brussels to Madrid. You have money saved up from your job last summer. Spend it on plane fare."

There were so many reasons why Alyssa's plan wouldn't work that I couldn't figure out where to begin. Asking Val's parents for an expensive present. Spending money I'd saved for college on a trip to Europe.

But what held me back from even fantasizing was my doubt that Lauren wanted to see me. When she first got to Spain, we e-mailed all the time. But I hadn't heard from her in more than a month, and that was after I'd e-mailed her three times, telling her what was going on in school. All she wrote back was that she loved Madrid and that her host family had asked if she could stay on with them through the summer and her parents had said yes. None of which sounded to me like she was in the mood for a drop-in visit from me.

"I'd better not," I said. "Mom'll be mad if I don't study during vacation."

"You could study on the plane," Alyssa said. "I do all the time."

"You don't study anywhere," Brooke said. "Besides, I have a better idea. Come with me to Maryland, Willa, for the dressage test. Alyssa's right about one thing. Gram's always saying what a nice girl you are. She'll listen if you tell her how I'm longing for a new horse."

"Longing?" I said.

Brooke laughed. "Gram likes a little drama," she replied. "Come on, Willa. Say yes. You and Terri and Gram and me for the weekend. It won't be Madrid, but it'll still be fun."

Brooke, I knew, would be having fun, since she'd be hanging out with her riding friends. But Mom would probably appreciate having me along, since it was hard for her to socialize with Val's parents.

"I'll ask Mom," I said.

Brooke hugged me. "Remember," she said, "I'm longing for that new horse. I won't survive freshman year without one."

"I'll remember," I said. "But I'll still miss Sweetbriar."

"Well, I'm not going to miss these sweaters," Brooke said. "I'll take them downstairs now. See you in the morning. Lyss, you be nice to Willa. I need her!"

Brooke left the room, waving the sweaters over her head. Alyssa went back to her laptop, and I tried to concentrate on my French.

Alyssa fell asleep first. She always did, exhausted from her tennis practices, her workouts, and her running. She didn't set the alarm, but I knew she'd wake up around five. She liked to jog for an hour before school. Maybe she'd get her homework done, and maybe not.

I lay in bed. I usually had trouble falling asleep. That night, like most others, I tried to synchronize my breathing with Alyssa's. Sometimes that worked. That night it didn't.

I was still awake when Jack and Mom came upstairs. I heard them knock softly on Brooke's door and whisper good night to her. They peeked in on Alyssa and me. I pretended, as I always did, to be asleep, so they wouldn't worry.

The lights went out, first in Mom and Jack's bedroom, then in Brooke's. I was alone, as I was so many nights, surrounded by my family but alone with my thoughts.

Everyone was asleep. I could get out of bed, leave my bedroom, walk quietly downstairs to the kitchen and then down to the basement, and go to my spot, my private spot by the furnace where I kept my razorblades and peroxide and bandages, all hidden where no one could find them.

Only a little cut, I told myself. A quick one on my left calf. A half inch long. Just enough to get me through the night.

Sometimes when I cut, I can't explain to myself why I need to. But that last time, five days earlier, I understood exactly what was going on.

I'd come home from choir practice to find the house was empty. Mom had left a note saying Alyssa was at tennis practice and Brooke had needed a lift to the riding academy.

I was glad to be alone. I had known as soon as I entered the house that I wasn't going to make it through the rest of the day without cutting.

Mrs. Chen, the choirmaster, had assigned solos for the spring concert. To my astonishment and delight, I'd been given one.

I thought about how excited Mom would be when I told her, and then I decided not to, to keep it secret until the concert itself. Jack loves surprises, and Mom would be thrilled, and Brooke and Alyssa would get a big kick out of it too.

Just picturing it, the solo and how my family would react, made me happier than I could ever remember being.

But after practice ended, Mrs. Chen drew me aside.

"You know I reserve the big solos for seniors at the spring concert," she said. "But you have a very special gift, Willa. I don't think you understand how good you could be."

"I love singing," I said. "Just being in the choir is wonderful."

"I don't want you to think I'm pushing you," Mrs. Chen said, then laughed. "All right. Maybe I am pushing a little. But I hate to see a talent like yours go to waste. Have you thought about getting a voice coach?"

I shook my head.

"There are so many excellent ones in Philadelphia," she said. "Where does Brooke get her violin lessons? Locally or in Philly?"

Brooke is first violinist for the school orchestra, so there was no way Mrs. Chen was unfamiliar with her. Still, her question surprised me.

"Locally," I said. "She's had the same teacher for years."

"I'm sure there are good local voice coaches," Mrs. Chen said. "But I really think you'd be in better hands with one in Philly. I can come up with a few recommendations if you'd like. How about if I talk to your parents about it?"

Westbridge High may not be a private school, but the kids here are rich. Their parents, like Val, earn hundreds of thousands of dollars, and the kids, like Brooke and Alyssa, take tennis and golf and dressage and music lessons.

But Jack earns maybe ten percent of that, and Mom doesn't get paid for looking after us. The money I'd earned last summer as an au pair was going to help pay for college.

I could understand why Mrs. Chen figured if there was money for Brooke's lessons there would be money for mine, but she was wrong, and I certainly didn't want to put Mom in the position of having to explain that.

"I'll ask my mother," I said, knowing I wouldn't. I'd learned a long time ago not to ask for the things I couldn't have.

I had never thought about voice lessons before Mrs. Chen suggested them. I should have been happy Mrs. Chen complimented me, excited to have the solo. I was lucky to go to a school with such a great choir.

I knew all of that, but I'd run to my private space in the basement anyway and cut my right thigh. I'd cut deeper than I'd intended, so it was a relief no one was home to hear when I cried out in pain. The kind of pain I needed to keep me from thinking about all the things I wanted and could never have.

Five days. My rule was never cut more than once a week, and better still to wait ten days or even two weeks. Last year there'd been a stretch when I'd gone seventeen days without cutting. I hadn't told myself I couldn't. I just hadn't felt the need.

I felt the need then, though, as I lay on my bed, listening to Alyssa's steady breathing. I felt the need as I thought about my happy family. But it had only been five days.

I closed my hands into the tightest fists possible, my fingernails pressing into my palms. It wasn't as good as cutting, but it was all I allowed myself.

That's what I remember from that night. The sweaters, the planning, the laughter, the invitations, the need.

three

I WAS THE FIRST ONE home from school. I usually was, since Brooke and Alyssa had so many more activities than I did, and Mom had either her classes or her chauffeuring. Jack wouldn't be back until after supper.

We keep two charts in the kitchen, one to remind everyone where we all were scheduled to be, and the other to tell us which chores we were expected to do around the house. The chores rotated, so we each had a week of them every month, regardless of other obligations (although we all traded on occasion). It was my week for dusting and vacuuming, and I figured I'd get to that after I'd checked for phone messages and before I began my homework.

That was what I was thinking about when I picked up the phone to see if there were any messages. Whether I should dust and vacuum before I did my homework or after.

There were four messages, all in the past two hours.

That was a lot, but not unheard of. We knew that if there were any last-minute changes in our schedules we were to call home and leave a message. Then whoever got in first could call Mom or Jack and let them know what was going on. Jack called the voice mail our bulletin board, and it was a pretty good system.

The first message was from Faye Parker, Mom's best friend since first grade. They live two thousand miles apart now, since Mom and I moved to Pennsylvania when I was four and Faye stayed at home in Pryor, Texas. Faye had visited Mom and me only once, when Jack took the girls to Shanghai for the first time, but she and Mom talked regularly.

"Terri, this is Faye. I'm at work and I can't find your cell number. Do me a favor and call when you get in. Thanks. It's kinda important."

We keep a pad by the phone in the kitchen. I wrote down, "Call Faye," and went to the second message.

"It's me again. Terri, I don't want you to get concerned or anything, but there's an Amber Alert for one of the twins.

I'm not sure what's going on, but I really need you to call me as soon as you get in."

Faye didn't have any kids, so I tried to figure out who the twin might be, and why Faye or Mom would care. It was possible Mom's brother, Martin, had twins. Martin and his wife live in Idaho, in some kind of cult. The last Mom heard, they had eight daughters, but since Martin thought Mom was an infidel for leaving her husband, he'd stopped talking to her. Martin's ten years older than Mom anyway, and they were never very close. He might have twins, although most of his daughters were older than I was, so I couldn't see why there'd be an Amber Alert for any of them. Maybe the twin was one of his grandkids; Mom figured he must have a boatload by now. I wasn't certain how Amber Alerts worked, but maybe they were national and Faye had heard about it somehow.

The third message was thirty minutes old. "Terri, call me as soon as you can. It sounds like Budge is in a lot of trouble. Have you heard from him? Just call me, okay?"

I underlined "Call Faye" three times and tried to figure out who Budge was. I didn't think it was any of Faye's exes or if it was, why Faye would think Mom would have heard from him.

I knew I wasn't going to like the fourth message. But I played it anyway.

"Terri, look, I've gotta talk to you. The news about Budge, it sounds really bad, and not hearing from you has got me worried. Call me the second you get in. I need to hear that you're all right. As soon as you get this message, call. I'm starting to go crazy."

I called Mom's cell. I got her voice mail.

"Mom, something's going on with Faye," I said. "Someone named Budge is in trouble, and there's an Amber Alert for a twin, and I have no idea what she's talking about. But call her, okay, and then call me?"

I hung up, and almost without thinking, I called her again. "Call me first," I said. "I'm home. Call here."

I realized then that I was shaking, like Faye's craziness had infected me. Someone I'd never heard of thousands of miles away was in some unknown trouble, and all I felt was terror.

I called Jack. He answered on the first ring.

"Jack, I'm scared," I said. "Something horrible has happened and I can't find Mom and I don't know what's going on."

"Where are you?" he asked. "Willa, are you all right?"

"I'm fine," I said. "It's Faye. She called Mom four times to tell her something bad's happened to someone named Budge. I don't understand any of it, but there's an Amber Alert for a twin and I guess this Budge person's involved, and Faye's really scared for Mom. I called Mom twice now, but she didn't pick up her cell, so I'm scared too." Just telling Jack all that made me feel better, made me feel foolish.

Jack said the right things. Jack always said the right things. "I need you to do two things," he said. "First, look on the chart and see where Terri is scheduled to be."

The chart was right in front of me. "Alyssa has practice from two to four," I said.

"All right," Jack said. "I'll call the club. It could be Terri turned off her cell. Now I need you to give me Faye's phone number."

"She's at work," I said. "Let me get her work number and her cell number."

"Do that," Jack said. "I'll call and find out what's going on."

I dug through the address book until I found both numbers. "Do you understand any of this?" I asked Jack, after I read him the numbers. "Do you know who Budge is?"

"No," Jack said. "Look, I'll find out from Faye what's going on, and I'll track Terri down, and then I'll get back to you. Meanwhile, try to get your homework done and don't worry. All right?"

"All right," I said. I hung up the phone and stood frozen with indecision. I knew I couldn't concentrate on homework or dusting. I wanted desperately to go to the basement, hide in my little corner, cut deep and hard before the pressure inside me exploded. But there's no phone in the basement and I didn't dare miss another call.

It's been less than a week, I told myself. *I can't cut anyway.*

I decided to pour myself a drink of water. I took a glass out from the cabinet, but my hands were shaking so hard, I dropped it. The glass shattered into a hundred pieces. I picked up the largest of the shards, and I can't be sure, but I think it was an accident when it cut into my palm. I was bleeding pretty hard, and the pain was intense, and that helped me focus. I went to the bathroom, cleaned the cut and bandaged it, then went to the kitchen and swept up the broken glass. When we'd first moved in together, Brooke went through a stage where she dropped things. She broke glasses and coffee cups and Mom's favorite vase. Alyssa never broke anything. I guess I fell somewhere between the two.

I had just finished throwing out the broken glass when the phone rang. I dropped the dustbin and ran to answer it.

"Sweetie, I don't want you to worry," Jack said. "I can't track your mother down, but that doesn't mean anything."

"Did you speak to Faye?" I asked. "What's going on?"

"I just got off the phone with her," Jack said.

The doorbell rang. "There's someone here," I said, not giving Jack a chance to say anything more. "Hold on."

I could hear him calling my name, but it didn't matter. I ran to the front door and opened it.

There were two police officers standing there, a man and a woman. They showed me their badges and their identification. "I'm Officer Schultz, and this is Officer Rivera," the man said. "May we come in?"

I thought, *There's been an accident. Mom's dead.*

Things started swirling around, and one of the cops caught me before I fell to the floor.

"Here, sit down," he said. "Put your head between your knees. That's right. Rivera, get her some water."

Rivera ran in the direction of the kitchen. I heard her pouring water into a glass. Within seconds, she was in the living room, helping me hold my head up while I took some sips.

"Are you all right?" she asked me. She must have noticed my bandaged palm. "Are you cut bad?"

"No," I said. "It was an accident." I swallowed hard, waiting to hear about another accident, a worse accident.

"We're looking for Terri McDougal," Officer Schultz said. "Are you her daughter?" He looked down at his clipboard. "Willa Coffey?"

"Yes," I said. "Why are you looking for her? Is she all right?"

"That's what we're trying to find out," Officer Rivera said. "When did you hear from her last?"

"This morning," I said. "Before school. My stepfather's trying to find her too." I remembered Jack was on the phone. "Oh," I said. "We were talking when you came. I'd better let him know you're here." I got up a little faster than I should have, and things got dizzy again.

"I'll talk to him," Officer Schultz said. He walked to the kitchen, and I could hear him saying something to Jack, then hanging up.

"Your sister is at her tennis lesson," he said, as he joined us in the living room. "Your mother dropped her off and said she'd be back around four o'clock to pick her up. No one knows where she went from there." He looked at his watch. "It's three thirty now," he said. "If she isn't there in half an hour, we'll start looking for her. Meantime, we'll keep you company."

"I don't understand any of this," I said. "Mom got some messages from her friend Faye about an Amber Alert and someone named Budge being in trouble. But why are you here?"

"A woman called our precinct and said she was worried that a man named Dwayne Coffey might be trying to get to your mother," Officer Rivera replied. "There's an APB out for him, so we took the call seriously."

"Dwayne Coffey is my father," I said. "Faye must have called. Look, if you don't mind, I'm going to call her."

"That's a good idea," Officer Schultz said. "We'll wait here."

I went to the kitchen, found Faye's cell number, and called. "Terri, is that you?" she asked, before I even could say hello.

"It's Willa," I said. "Faye, what's going on? There are two police officers here, and they said there's an APB for Dwayne Coffey. Only they won't tell me why. Who's Budge? What does the Amber Alert have to do with us?"

"Oh, sweetie, Budge is your daddy," Faye said. "That's his old nickname. When I couldn't get through to your momma, I called the police."

"But why would my father be trying to get here?" I asked. "Mom and I haven't seen him since we left Texas."

I could hear Faye inhale sharply. "Look, sweetie, I'm not the person to tell you," she said. "That's for your momma to do. Just have her call me as soon as you hear from her, so I can stop worrying, all right?"

"Faye!" I said, but she'd hung up. I called Jack, but I got his voice mail. There was no point leaving a message, so I hung up and went back to the living room.

"Budge is Dwayne Coffey's nickname," I said to the officers, who were still sitting there. "An APB means the police are looking for him, right? Did he kidnap someone? Is that why there's an Amber Alert?"

"Why don't we start with you first," Officer Schultz said. "When was the last time you heard from your father?"

"I never hear from him," I said. "He and my mother got divorced when I was little. Mom and Jack got married when I was five, and as far as I'm concerned, he's my father, not some guy I hardly remember. So you can tell me whatever you want about Dwayne Coffey, because he means nothing to me. Who did he kidnap? Who are the twins?"

The officers exchanged glances.

"We don't know much more than you do," Officer Rivera said. "There was a domestic disturbance at his house. Coffey and one of his daughters are missing."

I was a lot more shocked to hear my father had other daughters than I was to learn there'd been a domestic disturbance at his house. Mom never talked about what went on in Texas, but there had to be a reason why she'd run off with me.

"How many daughters does he have?" I asked. "Besides me, I mean."

They looked at each other again. "There were three little girls," Officer Schultz said.

"Were?" I repeated. "What do you mean there *were* three little girls? What kind of domestic disturbance was there?"

"Maybe we should wait until your mother gets home," Officer Rivera said.

The telephone rang. I jumped out of my chair and ran to the kitchen to answer it.

"Willa, it's Brooke. Daddy and I are on our way to the club," she said. "We're all right and Alyssa is too, and if Terri doesn't show up when she's supposed to, the police will start looking for her. Wait a second." I could hear her and Jack whispering, and then Brooke got back on. "Daddy wants to know if the cops are still there."

"Yes," I said.

I heard Brooke tell Jack that. "He says you should ask them to stay until he gets home," she said. "He'll call as soon as we get to the club, and you shouldn't worry."

"Tell him I'm fine," I said, knowing that was what Jack would want to hear.

"All right," Brooke said. "We'll call in a few minutes."

Talking to Brooke helped calm me down. I walked back to the living room and sat down. "That was my stepsister," I said. "She and Jack are on their way to the tennis club. That's where my other stepsister is. They're going to wait for my mother there."

"Good," Officer Rivera said. "We'll stay here until you hear back from them."

"We were talking about my sisters," I said. It felt so

[33]

strange, saying "sisters" and not meaning Brooke and Alyssa. "My father has three little girls? But Faye said the Amber Alert was for one of the twins. So there must be another twin and another girl, right? Are they okay? What about their mother? Why are the police looking for my father? Why are you here?"

"The bodies of a woman and two little girls were found at Dwayne Coffey's house," Officer Schultz said. "They were found earlier today. Dwayne Coffey and one of his daughters are missing."

I felt as though the whole house had been picked up by a tornado, that it and everything I'd ever known was twisting out of the solar system.

"We don't know that they're your sisters," Officer Rivera said. "They haven't been identified yet."

"But that's what the police think," I said. "If they're in his house, they're probably his daughters. Only he has three daughters."

"In that house," Officer Schultz said.

"Oh," I said. "He has four daughters, doesn't he? That's why Faye's hysterical. She thinks he's going from house to house, murdering his families. But Mom and I live thousands of miles away. He still lives in Texas, doesn't he?"

"Yes, he does," Officer Schultz said. "But the homicides seem to have happened a couple of days ago. There's no way of knowing where he and the other little girl are at this moment."

"So he could be coming here," I said. "I see."

Of course, I didn't see anything. You can't see anything when you feel like someone is punching you over and over again in the gut.

"It's too early in the investigation to draw conclusions," Officer Rivera said. She leaned over as she spoke and touched me gently on the hand I'd cut. "All that's known for sure is that a woman and two young children were found dead in a house your father lived in. One little girl seems to be missing, and no one knows where your father is. It could be he and the little girl escaped, and he's hiding somewhere until he's sure it's safe."

"Were they shot?" I asked. "The woman and the little girls." My stepmother. My half sisters. "Maybe the woman shot the girls and then shot herself."

"The report says there were a lot of stab wounds," Officer Schultz said. "Mrs. Coffey, if it is Mrs. Coffey, seems to be a victim, not a killer."

"Well, I wouldn't know," I said. "I don't know any of these people. I haven't seen my father since I was four. I don't even think of him as my father. If you'll excuse me, please, I'm not feeling very well."

I felt their eyes on me as I raced to the bathroom to throw

up. My palm throbbed. Every cut on my body, even the ones long healed, throbbed.

I love cuts. I love blood. If there had been razorblades in the bathroom, I would have cut every inch of my body.

But there were no razorblades in the bathroom. I splashed cold water on my face and told myself none of this was about me.

There was a knock on the door. "Willa, are you all right?" Officer Rivera asked.

"I'm fine," I said, drying my face with a hand towel and emerging clean and unbloody from the bathroom. Before I had more of a chance to prove how fine I was, the phone rang.

"I'll get it," I said, racing past Officer Rivera so I could get to the phone first.

"Willa?"

"Mom!" I cried. "Mom, are you all right?"

"Honey, I'm fine," she said. "I went to the library and turned my cell off. I'm at the club with Jack and the girls. Jack said Faye was worried about me. Could you call her, let her know I'm all right?"

Mom doesn't know, I thought. *Jack hasn't told her.*

"I'll call Faye," I said. "Will you be home soon?"

"Jack and I are coming straight home," Mom replied. "Brooke's taking my car. She and Alyssa are stopping off at a friend's house."

"Okay," I said. "Great. Come on home. I'll call Faye."

"Thanks, honey," Mom said. "See you in a few minutes."

"That was my mother," I said to Officer Rivera as I hung up. "Jack is bringing her home. She was at the library. You don't have to wait if you don't want to. They'll be here in a few minutes."

"We'll wait," Officer Rivera said, giving me a smile. "We're in no hurry."

"All right," I said. Most likely Jack planned to tell Mom whatever it was he knew as they drove home. Or maybe the police officers would tell her, but Jack would be there when they did. Maybe Mom would be able to convince the cops that my father couldn't possibly be involved. Maybe she could explain to me how it was that I had three half sisters and she hadn't felt the need to tell me.

"I have to call Faye," I said. "Mom asked me to."

"Of course," Officer Rivera said. She left me alone in the kitchen.

I dialed Faye's number. "It's Willa," I said. "I just spoke to Mom. She's fine. Jack's bringing her home."

"Thank you, Jesus," Faye said.

"She doesn't know yet," I said. "About . . . about Budge. About the bodies. I think Jack'll tell her, or maybe the police will. She might be too upset to call you for a while. But she's fine. You don't have to worry anymore."

"Thank you, Willa," Faye said. "I'm sure you'll be a great comfort."

"I'll try," I said. "Uh, Faye?"

"Yes, sweetie?"

"Mom knew? I mean, that he had gotten married again and had kids?"

"She knew," Faye said. "But, sweetie, it wasn't important. You're all that matters to her, you and Jack and the girls."

"I wondered," I said, "because she never told me."

"Your momma was just trying to protect you." I could hear her start to cry. "You be there for her," she said. "She's going to need you."

I hung up and returned to the living room. "I was supposed to dust and vacuum," I said to the officers. "I guess there's no point starting now. Mom and Jack'll be home soon."

"I hate vacuuming," Officer Schultz said. "That's the one job I won't do. Dishes, diapers even, I don't mind. But my wife does all the vacuuming."

"I don't mind vacuuming," Officer Rivera said. "What I hate is throwing out the garbage."

"Well, we see enough garbage on the job," Officer Schultz said.

"More than enough," Officer Rivera said.

"I don't like throwing out garbage either," I said. "Could you excuse me, please? I'm going to be sick again."

This time, when Officer Rivera knocked on the door to see if I was all right, I told her I was but I didn't come out. I guess she figured I couldn't get into much trouble in a bathroom, because she left me alone after that, and I stayed in there until I heard the car pulling up in our driveway.

I met Mom and Jack at the back door. Jack was holding Mom up, helping her walk into the house. "The officers are in the living room," I said. "They've been waiting for you."

Jack reached over and gave me an awkward embrace. "How are you, pumpkin?" he asked.

"I'm fine," I said.

"Do me a favor and pour your mother a brandy," he said. "Bring it to the living room."

"Okay," I said.

"I'm all right, honey," Mom said. "I was feeling a little faint, that's all."

"I know," I said. "I'll join you in a minute."

Mom seemed sturdier and she managed to walk to the living room without holding on to Jack. I went to the dining room, found the brandy and the snifters, and poured one for Mom.

"I sent my daughters to a friend's house," Jack was saying as I joined them. "As a precaution."

"That's a good idea," Officer Rivera said. "I'm sure they're in no danger, but it might be better if they stayed away from here for the time being."

"What about Terri and Willa?" Jack asked.

"We'd like to talk to Mrs. McDougal first, if we could," Officer Schultz said. "Any information we could convey to the Texas police would help. After that, the safest thing would be for you all to move in to a motel. Just as a precautionary measure."

"When was the last you heard from Dwayne Coffey?" Officer Rivera asked.

Mom took a sip of her brandy. "About four years ago," she replied. "Right after we moved here. I wrote Budge to ask if he'd let Jack adopt Willa. That's his nickname: Budge. He wrote back a very abusive letter. He said I'd only written to extort money from him. Which I hadn't. When we got the divorce, I signed away any claims for alimony or child support, and I've never asked him for a penny."

"You didn't tell me you'd written Dwayne," Jack said.

"Things were so crazy then," Mom said. "The move. Val leaving. If Budge had said okay, I would have told you. He didn't, so I kept it to myself."

"Willa told us she's had no contact with him," Officer Rivera said. "Not since she was a little girl. Did he ever say he wanted to see her? Maybe in that letter?"

"No," Mom said. "I don't know what I would have done

if he had. When I was with Budge, he was always promising to turn over a new leaf, but he never did. But Faye told me he'd accepted Jesus as his savior and was working steady. She'd see him in church every Sunday. He and his wife had a little daughter and newborn twin girls. I thought now that he had three daughters, maybe he'd be ready to let Willa go."

"But his letter disturbed you," Officer Rivera said. "Did he threaten you?"

"No," Mom said. "It was more his tone than anything. It brought back a lot of bad memories. I only read it once, and then I threw it out."

"When you were married, had he been abusive?" Officer Rivera asked. "To you or Willa?"

Mom glanced at me, then looked away. "Budge and I both had tempers," she said. "It was a bad marriage. When I couldn't take it anymore, I grabbed Willa and ran."

"All right," Officer Schultz said, putting away his notebook. "I think you should pack a couple of days' worth of clothes, just to be on the safe side. I'm sure this will be wrapped up by then."

"Let us know what motel you're staying at," Officer Rivera said. "In case we need to reach you."

"Wait a second," Mom said. "There's one more thing."

We all stared at her.

"Trace," she said. "Budge's son, Trace. He's a couple years

older than Willa. The Texas police probably know about him already."

"Do you have any idea how we could find him?" Officer Schultz asked.

Mom shook her head. "I don't even know what last name he goes by," she said. "Coffey or Sheldon. And Mandy, his mother, has been married a couple of times, so I don't know what her last name is either."

"Do you think your friend Faye would know where Trace is?" Officer Rivera asked.

"I doubt it," Mom said. "She hasn't mentioned him in years. Mandy was in Georgia, the last I heard. Maybe he's with her. Maybe he enlisted. Maybe he's in jail." She turned away from the others and faced me, looked straight into my eyes. "Trace is what you would have been," she said, "if Jack hadn't rescued us both."

four

To my surprise, Jack drove us to Curt and Pauline Henderson's house. Curt and Pauline had both worked at the paper with Jack, and he'd stayed close with them after they retired.

When Jack had said Brooke and Alyssa were at a friend's, I assumed it was a friend of Brooke's. But Jack had told them to go to the Hendersons' and wait there until they heard from him.

"You'd better come in," Jack said to Mom and me. "It's safer."

"Budge isn't going to find us sitting in the Hendersons' driveway," Mom said.

"Terri, please," Jack said.

Mom and I got out of the car and followed Jack to the door. Curt opened it before Jack had a chance to ring the bell.

"We've been keeping an eye out for you," Curt said. "Come on in."

We found Brooke and Alyssa sitting in the living room. "Pauline's in the kitchen, making sandwiches," Curt said. "In case you're hungry."

"I couldn't eat anything," Mom said. "Willa?"

I shook my head. "No, thanks," I said.

"You can stop making the sandwiches," Curt called to Pauline. I guess she stopped, because she came into the living room.

"Terri, I'm so sorry," she said, giving Mom a hug. "Come here, Willa. This must be awful for you."

I love Curt and Pauline. Jack's parents are very nice, but I can tell they feel differently about me than they do Brooke and Alyssa. And Mom's parents died a couple of years after we'd left Texas. Curt and Pauline are more like grandparents than any I've ever had.

Brooke and Alyssa both looked uncomfortable. "We spoke to Mom," Brooke said.

"She says you have to take us to Orlando, Daddy," Alyssa said. "She says it's the safest place for us until they catch Willa's father, but we shouldn't fly there alone."

"She was pretty insistent, Dad," Brooke said. "I think you'd better call her."

"Excuse me," Jack said, and left the room. He went to the den and closed the door.

"Are you all right?" Brooke asked me.

"I'm fine," I said. For all I knew, I was. "As soon as I heard from Mom, I felt better."

"What a horrible, horrible thing for all of you," Pauline said. "I can't even imagine."

I couldn't either, maybe because none of it felt real, except for the throbbing pain in my palm. "I broke a glass," I said. "I dropped it and it shattered. I swept it all up, but one of the shards cut me."

"Is it a bad cut?" Mom asked. "Should you see a doctor?"

"No," I said. "I put peroxide on it and a bandage. It's no big deal."

Brooke gave me a funny look. I wondered if she knew I cut. I was careful not to let anything show, but it was always possible Alyssa had seen something while I was changing and mentioned it to Brooke.

"Are you sure you don't want something to eat?" Pauline asked. "Or drink? How about if I made some tea?"

"Not for me, thank you," Mom said.

Jack came back to the living room. "Val says she won't stop worrying until the girls are under her roof," he told us. "Her secretary got us seats on the nine fifteen flight. I'll spend the night in Orlando and get a morning flight home."

I caught Curt and Pauline exchanging glances, but Mom didn't notice. She and Jack hardly ever fight. Jack hates scenes and Mom hates upsetting Jack. "We'll be fine," she said. "And once the girls are with Val, you won't have to worry about them."

"How long will we be there?" Alyssa asked. "Spring vacation's in a couple of weeks. Maybe I should go to Munich with Mom. I could go to Brussels from there."

Jack shook his head. "This will all be resolved in a day or two," he said. "You'll be back in school by Monday."

Curt looked uncomfortable. "I don't know how long it's going to take them to catch Coffey," he said. "These Amber Alerts seem to be very effective. But the story may have legs."

"Why?" Mom asked. "Dwayne's a nobody from Nowhere, Texas. Why should anyone care?"

"It's the missing-kid aspect," Curt said. "Two children dead, one missing. A twin, at that. Missing twins and murder is a potent combination for cable news."

"We'll worry about that if it happens," Jack said. "Meantime, we'd better go back home and pack some clothes."

"Terri and Willa are welcome to stay here," Pauline said. "For as long as it takes."

"That's sweet of you," Mom said. "But the police suggested we go to a motel. I think Jack is right, and this will all blow over in a day or two. Budge'll probably get pulled over for drunk driving and they'll find his little girl sleeping in the back seat."

"Who's Budge?" Alyssa asked.

"Dwayne," Mom said. "Dwayne Coffey. My miserable no-good ex."

"My daddy," I said.

"Don't you ever call him that," Mom said. "Ever."

Jack looked miserable. Not that any of us looked happy.

"We'll take my car to the motel," Curt said. "I'll use my charge card to check Terri and Willa in. I doubt Coffey'll be calling motels to try to find you, but why take chances."

"Thanks," Jack said. "Better safe than sorry."

Well, we were all sorry. Just sorry for different things.

five

"Is there anything you want to talk about?" Mom asked. "Do you have any questions?"

"No," I said.

We were in the motel room. It was a suite, actually, a living room with a sofa bed and a bedroom. Mom said she'd sleep in the living room. I guess she saw herself as a line of defense in case Dwayne Budge-Not-Daddy Coffey showed up, knife in hand.

"Yeah," I said. "I do have a question. Why do you and Faye call him Budge? I've never heard you call him that. Jack didn't even know who Budge was when I asked him."

"It's his nickname," Mom said. "He was so stubborn. You know, he'd never budge an inch. Granny Coffey named him that. I don't know what people call him now. Probably Dwayne."

I couldn't remember if I'd ever heard Mom talk to Faye about anyone named Budge. If she had, I probably assumed it was another one of Faye's crazy exes.

"Is that all?" Mom asked. "I know this must be very hard for you, very confusing. You've never really asked me about Dwayne. I've liked to think that's because you feel Jack is your father. He is, in every way that counts."

"Except biologically," I said. "And legally."

"Legally wasn't his choice," Mom said. "Dwayne wouldn't give permission. He wouldn't budge."

"But couldn't you have sued him or something?" I asked. "How could he have any legal rights if he didn't have any contact with me?"

"I'd hear from him," Mom said. "Around your birthday usually. A couple of times at Christmas. A couple of times for no occasion. He'd send a little money to buy you a present."

"What did you do with the money?" I asked.

"What do you think I did with it?" Mom snapped back. "Bought myself diamonds? If the money came before your birthday, before Christmas, I bought you a present. If the money came too late, I used it on clothes for you. Trust me, ten bucks once or twice a year doesn't go very far."

"But he remembered me," I said. "He remembered my birthday. And you didn't tell me."

"Don't second-guess me right now," Mom said. "Just don't, Willa. I'm exhausted and I don't need that. In a good year, he remembered you twice. Jack remembered you every single day. Jack read to you at night and chased away your nightmares and cried at your middle-school graduation. Jack's been a wonderful father to you."

"I love Jack," I said. "You know I do. It's just . . ."

"It's just what?" Mom said. "That you feel deprived because I kept you from your drunken, murdering daddy?"

"I do have another question," I said. "Do I look like Budge? Is that who I look like?"

"Yes, you do," Mom said. "You have his mouth. You have his eyes."

six

I woke up early the next morning, peeked into the living room area, and saw Mom sleeping on the sofa. She hadn't even opened the mattress, just stretched out on the sofa and slept there instead.

There was no way of knowing when she'd fallen asleep. It wasn't like we'd sat around chatting. I'd gone into my room and she'd stayed in hers, and we both watched TV. Different shows, though.

I tiptoed back to my bedroom and turned the TV on to one of the cable news networks. It took about twenty minutes before the early-morning anchor said, "There's a new development in the story we've been covering of four-year-old Krissi Coffey, missing since the murder of her mother and two sisters in the small town of Pryor, Texas, two days ago. It was reported that a man fitting the description of Krissi's father, Dwayne Coffey, was seen taking a young child into a restroom at a gas station in Clayton, Ohio, late last night."

They showed a picture, like one of those Sears family portraits, of three little girls. *My sisters,* I thought. Three little blond girls, one slightly older than the other two. None of them had my mouth, my eyes.

"It's uncertain if the man was Dwayne Coffey, a person of interest in the murder of his wife and two of his children, or if the little girl was Krissi Coffey."

They showed a police officer then, saying, "We can confirm the deaths of Crystal Danielle Coffey, age twenty-five, her daughters Kelli Marie, age six, and Kadi Coffey, age four. Her husband, Dwayne Coffey, age thirty-seven, is wanted for questioning."

They cut then to a picture of Dwayne Budge-Not-Daddy Coffey. The man with my mouth, my eyes.

It was some kind of ID picture, but not a mug shot. Not a great picture, but you could see what he looked like, if not who he was.

Mom had been right. I did look like him. The shape of

our faces, the way our mouths turned down so we always look sad even when we aren't.

Maybe he was sad. I had no way of knowing.

"Willa?"

I turned off the TV, feeling as guilty as if I'd committed a crime.

"I'm here, Mom," I said, opening the door and showing her that I was still alive, still part of her life.

"I heard the TV," she said. "Were you watching the news?"

"Yes, Mom," I said. "They may have spotted them in Ohio. A man took a little girl to a restroom in Ohio."

"Men take their little daughters to restrooms all the time," Mom said. "Why assume it's them?"

"I don't know, Mom," I said. "They have pictures of them. I guess they've been showing the pictures on TV, and someone saw them."

"What does he look like?" Mom asked. "I haven't seen him in ten years."

"He looks like me," I said.

"That's not what I mean," Mom said. "Is he clean-shaven? Does he have a beard, a mustache? The last time I saw him, he had a mustache."

"Clean-shaven," I said. "Didn't Faye keep you up to date on that stuff?"

But before Mom had a chance to tell me what she and Faye talked about when they talked about Budge, the telephone rang. We both jumped at the sound.

"That's probably Jack," Mom said, but I could tell from her end of the conversation that it wasn't. She said "Yes" a few times, and "I see" and "I understand," but not much else.

"That was the police," she told me as she hung up. "They're sending a detective over later to interview me."

"Why?" I asked. "You haven't seen him in ten years."

"They're taking that Ohio report pretty seriously," Mom replied. "The town where they saw him was on Route Seventy."

"They really think he's coming here?" I asked. "To see me?"

"It wouldn't be a social call," Mom said. "Get dressed, Willa. I'm going to call Jack, and then I'll take a shower. The detective won't be coming for an hour. We'll order room service. I don't know about you, but I'm hungry."

I hadn't eaten anything since I'd thrown up, and I still felt more queasy than hungry. But there was no point starving to death before I got to meet my father, who apparently was on his way over to kill me.

I went to the bathroom and took a quick shower. I looked around the bathroom to see if the motel provided razorblades. There weren't any, although there was a little card that said if I needed any, or a comb, or a toothbrush, I should just call room service. It was nice to have that as an option, although I couldn't see doing it with Mom five feet away.

Instead, I carefully peeled the bandage off my palm and rammed my fingernails into the cut. The pain was sharp enough to race through my whole body. I gasped, but Mom didn't hear. I put the bandage back on and finished getting dressed.

"Jack spent the night at Val's," Mom said. "Not much of a night. Their flight was delayed, and they didn't get to Orlando until after midnight. Then their cabdriver got lost, so they didn't get to her place until nearly two. Val wants Jack to be there when the girls wake up."

"But he's coming back," I said.

"Of course he is," Mom said. "He'll be here before supper. With any luck, we'll be home by then."

"Mom?" I said.

"What?"

"Did you ever love Budge?" I asked. *Would I have loved him?* I couldn't ask.

"I told myself I did," Mom said. "But I had no idea what love was until I met Jack. I'm taking my shower. Don't answer the phone or open the door. I'll call room service after I get dressed. That should time out pretty well."

She gathered her clothes and walked into the bathroom. I turned the TV on and watched pictures of my father and my sisters and a gas station in Ohio scroll over and over again.

seven

MOM, CURT, AND PAULINE were playing canasta. Mom didn't know how, so they taught her. They offered to teach me too, but I wasn't interested. I'm not sure Mom was either, but we appreciated that Curt and Pauline had given up whatever their plans for the day were to keep us entertained. They brought a pile of magazines, and I was leafing through them, keeping half an eye on the cable news station. They didn't have any new information about Budge or Krissi, but that didn't stop them from obsessing over the story. They showed an interview with Crystal's father, threatening to kill the murderer of his daughter and granddaughters with his bare hands. They showed another interview, this one with Crystal's sister begging Dwayne to return with little Krissi. Then they interviewed a former FBI profiler about what sort of man kills his wife and children, and why he might select one daughter to live. He was followed by a criminal pathologist, who explained what kind of damage multiple knife wounds could cause.

They showed Kelli Marie's kindergarten teacher and Pastor Hendrick of the New Hope Gospel Church, where my father and his wife and my three little sisters used to go every Sunday. By midafternoon, they'd pretty much shown the entire population of Pryor, except for maybe Faye.

Mom looked up a couple of times, mostly when they showed Pryor. "It looks worse than I remember," she said. "Deader somehow."

"It's hard for those little towns to survive," Curt said. "There are plenty of small towns in Pennsylvania, Ohio, even New York, like that."

"Things were bad with Dwayne," Mom said. "But what really scared me was Willa growing up in that miserable place. I think if Dwayne and I had moved when I asked him to, I would have stuck with him. At least for a little while longer."

"How did you end up here?" Pauline asked. "At the newspaper? Meeting Jack?"

"I grabbed Willa one day," Mom said. "I packed some clothes and searched through the house for any money—spare change, anything. Dwayne drank pretty hard, so he was careless about money. I'd saved a few dollars over the weeks and I'd lifted a twenty from my father's wallet. I took all the money and put it in a sandwich bag and dragged Willa and my overnight bag to the bus station. I kept the twenty and handed the cashier all the rest and asked her for tickets to as far from Pryor as we could get. It took a few months of moving around before we ended up here."

"That was very brave of you," Pauline said.

Mom shrugged. "Brave and dumb," she said. "But it all worked out."

By that point I'd seen the photograph of my father and the one of my sisters so often, I felt as though I knew them. I wished they'd show a picture of Trace so I'd get to "meet" my brother also, but they didn't mention him by name, or me. Just that Coffey had two older children and it was believed he might be en route to see one or both of them.

"Do you know where Trace lives?" Pauline asked Mom.

Mom shook her head. "Trace bounced around a lot," she said. "His mother. Budge and me. Foster care. The last I heard he was living with Budge's grandma, but he took off, or maybe she threw him out. That was maybe four years ago. Faye hasn't mentioned him since."

I thought about the message board in our kitchen, where we all wrote down our schedules for the week. Tennis lessons. Lacrosse practices. Choir rehearsals. Study dates and trips to the mall. Every minute accounted for. Even Val's business trips were listed.

"Maybe Dwayne heard from him," Pauline said. "Maybe Trace's in Ohio and that's why Dwayne drove there."

"Assuming it was Dwayne," Curt said, "and not some poor guy who was driving around last night for a completely innocent reason."

We sat there, playing cards, leafing through magazines, looking up at the TV more when there was a commercial than when there was news. Sometimes there'd be a reported sighting of Budge and Krissi, but the only one that had credence was the gas station in Ohio.

A criminal psychologist came on to discuss why Budge had stabbed his family rather than shooting them. Assuming he had, of course—which we all did.

"Stabbing is a more intimate way of killing," the psychologist said.

Mom looked up from her cards and snorted. "That's such crap," she said. "Budge was terrified of guns. Probably the only person in the Texas panhandle who wouldn't touch one. His daddy died in a hunting accident when Budge was seven. Shotgun went off and blew his head to bits. Budge saw the whole thing."

"That's horrible," Pauline said.

"Most likely he was drunk," Mom said. "Probably never knew what hit him. Budge used to say his momma left before the body was cold. Budge's granny raised him. She had her share of shotguns, rifles, but Budge wouldn't go near them. Everyone teased him, so he got real good with a knife. Nothing intimate about it. He just didn't own a gun."

"They have a lot of time to fill," Curt said. "Twenty-four-hour news. They interview any so-called expert they can find."

"I'm glad Jack covers sports, then," Mom said. "Clean and easy. A score is a score."

Curt grinned. "It's not always that simple," he said. "Nothing is."

Jack got to the motel room around five. We still had the TV on, but nothing new had been reported.

"I called the police from the airport," he said. "They're pretty sure it was Dwayne and his daughter at the gas station in Ohio, but there haven't been any other sightings they trust."

"How long do they think you should stay here?" Pauline asked.

"Checkout time tomorrow is eleven," Jack said. "They'll let us know if it's safe for us to go back home then."

"Will you have to go back to Orlando to get the girls?" I asked.

Jack shook his head. "They can fly home by themselves," he said. "They've done it before. Curt, Pauline, I can't thank you enough for staying with Terri and Willa. I worried a lot less knowing they weren't alone."

"Our pleasure," Pauline said. "But now, if you don't need us, we'll go home."

We exchanged farewell hugs. I was sorry to see them go, but I was relieved Jack was with us. It might not have been rational, but I felt more protected with him around.

"I told the girls I'd call them when I got here," he said, pulling out his cell phone. "They're a little jumpy because of everything. Hi, Brooke. Yes, I'm back. The flight was fine, much better than last night's. No, nothing new. Yeah, Sunday, Monday at the latest. I'll know better tomorrow, and I'll tell your mother. Where's Alyssa? Oh, all right. Yes, she's right here. Hold on." He handed the phone to me.

"Willa, how are you?" Brooke asked.

"Fine," I said. "Bored. You'll be back this weekend?"

"That's what Dad says," Brooke replied. "Monday at the latest. Willa, have you checked your messages?"

"No," I said. "Why?"

"I've gotten a lot of calls and texts," Brooke said. "A lot.

Some at lunchtime, and nonstop since school ended. My friends. A few of your friends. They're all worried about you."

"They know?" I asked.

"It's all over the news," Brooke said. "You having the same last name and Dwayne driving east from Ohio. Someone made the connection. I told everyone you were fine, but I couldn't tell them where you were." She laughed, but I could hear the embarrassment in her voice. "A few kids thought that was kind of exciting," she said. "Like you were undercover. But most of them just wanted to know if you were okay."

"I don't think I'm supposed to use my cell," I said, having no idea if that was true or not. "In case anyone can trace me from it."

"That makes sense," Brooke said. "Well, I'll tell everyone I spoke to you, and you should be in school on Monday."

Up until then, I'd been looking forward to getting back to school. If I were home and in school, it would feel as though none of this were real.

But that was before I'd realized people would know what had happened. And I'd go from being that quiet girl who happens to be Brooke McDougal's stepsister to being the daughter of a killer.

I handed the phone back to Jack and pulled out my

cell. I had seventeen messages and twice that many texts. Three of the messages were from Lauren. Someone must have let her know what was going on and she felt my father murdering his family was important enough to get in touch. I rammed my cell back in my bag.

Mom looked at me. "It'll be all right," she said. "I promise."

"I know," I said, because I didn't want her or Jack to be any more upset. Besides, a mother and two little girls were dead. What difference did it make if I was embarrassed?

eight

THE PHONE RANG.

The sound woke me up, and it took a while before I understood what was going on. I was in the motel bedroom, with Jack and Mom on the sofa bed in the living room area. It was three forty-five in the morning and something very bad must have happened.

No one calls at three forty-five A.M. with good news.

Mom opened the bedroom door and peeked in.

"I'm awake," I said, which was half true. "What is it?"

"I'm not sure," Mom said. "There are two police officers coming up. Do you think you can go back to sleep?"

"No," I said, climbing out of the bed and putting on my robe. "Do you know why they're here?"

"The desk clerk called," Mom said. "To let us know they were on their way up and that he'd checked their ID."

Jack was sitting on the opened sofa bed, talking on his cell. "I just wanted to be certain," he said. "Yes, it's better to be safe. Thank you." He hung up. "They're cops, all right," he said. "But I still don't know what's going on."

We could hear their footsteps coming down the hallway to our suite. "It can't be anything about Brooke and Alyssa," I said. "They're in Orlando."

"I'm sure they're fine," Mom said. "Most likely they found Budge and they're coming to tell us we can go home tomorrow."

They knocked quietly on the door. Jack got up and opened it.

The officers were in uniform. They introduced themselves and showed Jack their badges and ID. Mom and I sat on the sofa bed while Jack and the officers stood there.

"There's no easy way of saying this," Officer Washington said. "We have reason to believe your ex-husband is dead, ma'am. It would be a big help to us if you came down to the hospital and identified him."

"He's here?" Mom asked. "He came here?"

Officer Myers nodded.

"The little girl?" I asked. "My sister." For a moment, I couldn't remember her name. "Krissi. Did they find her?"

"I'm afraid she's dead also," Officer Washington said.

Mom gasped.

"What happened?" Jack asked.

"There was an incident," Officer Myers replied. "It's under investigation."

"Look," Jack said. "I can turn on the TV and find out exactly what's going on. Or you can stop beating around the bush and tell us what we need to know. We're talking about Willa's father and sister. We have a right to hear what happened."

"I'm sorry," Officer Washington said. "But before we go on, can you confirm your home address?"

"Twenty-two Cedar Lane, Westbridge," Mom said. "Why?"

"A man believed to be Dwayne Coffey approached your house," Officer Washington said. "The house was under surveillance, in case he showed up. A police officer approached him and asked for identification and the man attacked him with a knife. The officer's partner shot him. The attacker was taken to the hospital, but he died in the ambulance, presumably from the gunshot wounds."

"Oh my God," Mom said. "He was going to kill us."

"We don't know that, ma'am," Officer Washington said. "We don't even know for certain it was your ex-husband."

"The cop that was attacked," Jack said. "Is he all right?"

"He's expected to live," Officer Washington said.

"Krissi," I said. "You said she was dead too."

Officer Myers nodded. "She was found in the car," she said. "Wrapped in a blanket on the floor of the back seat."

"Stabbed?" Jack asked.

"Her head was severed," Officer Washington said. "I am sorry, ma'am, that we have to tell you this. Do you think you're up to making the identifications?"

"I can't identify the girl," Mom said. "I've never seen her."

"But you do remember what Dwayne Coffey looks like?" Officer Myers said.

"Yes," Mom said. "I do. Hold on. I'll change into some clothes and come with you."

"I'll come too," Jack said.

"No," Mom said. "You stay with Willa." She grabbed some clothes and went to the bathroom to change.

"They're really all dead?" I asked. "He came to our house and you killed him?"

Officer Washington looked at me. "She's in shock," he said. "Maybe you should take her to the emergency room."

"No," I said. "I'm okay."

Jack walked over and wrapped a blanket around me. "There'll be reporters all over the hospital," he said. "Will you be able to get Terri in and out without them seeing?"

"We'll do our best," Officer Washington said. "And we'll see if we can find a doctor to make a house call here."

"Thank you," Jack said. Or at least I think he said thank you. Because that's the kind of family I come from. We're very polite. Even when people die on our doorsteps, we remember to say please and thank you and excuse me.

nine

IT WAS ALMOST NOON when I woke up, and I was startled to find Mom asleep on the other side of the bed.

I tiptoed to the bathroom, splashed some cold water on my face, and groggily made my way to the living room. Jack was sitting at the table with Curt and Pauline. The room smelled of freshly brewed coffee.

I saw an open box of Danish and grabbed one. Pauline handed me a napkin.

Something about that gesture made me remember. Budge had been killed in front of our house the night before. Krissi, the last of my half sisters, was dead. What was it the officer had said? Her head severed.

I ran to the bathroom and threw up. When I finally emerged, I saw Mom was still sleeping.

"The doctor gave both of you sedatives," Jack said. "You were asleep by the time Terri got back."

"The cop," I said. "The one Budge cut."

"He's fine," Pauline said. "Treated and released."

"Budge came to our house," I said. "Did he come to kill us? If we'd been there, if the cops hadn't . . . would he have killed us all?"

"It doesn't matter," Jack said. "We weren't there, and the police were, and it's all over."

"There's a way some people choose to die," Curt said. "Suicide by cop. They do things that force police officers to kill them. I think that's what happened last night. Budge had enough of killing. He was ready to die."

"You make it sound so noble," Jack said.

Curt shook his head. "He was insane," he said. "He'd obviously lost all grip on reality. Maybe he meant to kill all of you. Maybe he was bringing Krissi as some kind of offering. We'll never know. But you're right about one thing, Jack. It's over. That's what's important. The nightmare is over, and you'll be able to get your lives back, as though this had never happened."

I thought, *We'll be a happy family again. My mother, my stepfather, my stepsisters, my half brother I've never met, my slaughtered stepmother and half sisters, my insane father killed by police bullets in my front yard. That's the life I'll be getting back.*

I would have burst out laughing, but I was afraid of how they'd react if I did. Instead I bit hard on the inside of my mouth, until the intensity of the pain let me get back under control.

"Brooke," I said. "Alyssa. Do they know?"

Jack nodded. "Alyssa woke up early, went online, and found out what happened before I had a chance to call," he replied. "Val's angry because I didn't tell her right away." He paused. "If I had, if I'd called Val in the middle of the night, that would have upset her just as much. But it would have been better for the girls. I didn't want Alyssa and Brooke to find out this way."

"There's no good way to find out something like this," Pauline said. "Willa, why don't you shower and get dressed. Maybe you'll feel up to eating after you've freshened up."

I did as she suggested. Even after I rejoined them, Mom was still sleeping.

"It's almost one," I said. "We missed the checkout time."

"We can't go home now anyway," Jack said. "Our house is a crime scene. The police are still there, and so are the reporters."

I noticed the TV set was off. "Is it on TV?" I asked. "Budge? Our house?"

Pauline nodded. "There's no reason for you to see any of it," she said. "They're not going to tell us anything we don't already know."

"Please," I said, thinking if I saw our front yard, our house, on the news, I might be able to believe what had happened there.

"No," Jack said. "Maybe later, Willa. I don't want you to see it now."

I knew Jack felt he was protecting me. That's what Jack did, protect me, protect Brooke and Alyssa, protect Mom. Even when we didn't want to be protected, he did it anyway.

"Is it in the papers?" I asked.

"Some," Curt said. "There'll be more tomorrow. It happened so late last night, it missed the deadline."

Deadline, I thought. *A line of the dead.* This time I did laugh.

"You need something to eat," Pauline said. "Something more nutritious than Danish. Fresh air would do you good too. Why don't I take you out for brunch?"

"Is that such a good idea?" Curt asked. "What if someone spots Willa?"

"We'll go to the Bright Star," Pauline said, naming a diner a half hour away. "We'll be gone a couple of hours. By

[73]

the time we get back, Terri'll be awake, and she and Jack will have had a chance to talk."

"Are you up for it?" Jack asked me. "Getting out of here for a couple of hours?"

I had no idea what I was up for, but I did sense I could talk to Pauline in a way I couldn't to Jack or Mom. I nodded.

"Good," Pauline said, grabbing her jacket and mine. "We'll see you in a while. Call if there's something you want us to get while we're out."

It felt strange to walk out of the motel suite and ride the elevator down to the lobby. I'd been in the suite for less than two days, but it was starting to feel like I'd spent my whole life there.

"Thanks for suggesting lunch out," I said. "I don't care where we go, just as long as it isn't here."

But Pauline was already pushing me back into the elevator. "Reporters," she whispered. "Checking in."

We rode the elevator back up in silence. My exciting expedition had lasted two minutes.

"No one saw us," Pauline told Jack and Curt as we took our jackets off and settled back in. "But I couldn't risk having Willa walk across the lobby to the parking lot. I knew a couple of the guys checking in. Even if they didn't recognize Willa, they would have spotted me."

"Well, it was worth the try," Jack said.

"I can slip out later," Curt said. "Get us something to eat. The reporters won't be in the lobby very long. They'll be going to the police station, to the crime scene."

"My home," Jack said. "The crime scene."

"That's what they do," Curt said. "But by the time they get back tonight, the three of you should be out of here."

"You can stay with us for as long as you need to," Pauline said.

Jack thought about it. "Today's Saturday," he said. "Sunday's a slow news day, so it'll be front page around here. Maybe some coverage on Monday, especially if they get their hands on Terri or Willa."

"These things burn out fast," Curt said. "The local crews will lose interest soon. The cable guys might go to Texas for the funerals, but that should be it."

"Val could send the girls home Tuesday," Jack said. "Wednesday at the latest. We'd be out of your hair by then. Willa could even go back to school Tuesday."

"That might be pushing it," Curt said. "But Wednesday for sure."

"No!" I said.

They stared at me, as though they'd never heard the word *no* before.

"My sisters died," I said.

"Your sisters are fine," Jack said. "They're in Orlando, with Val. You'll see them in a few days."

"My blood sisters," I said, remembering with the sting of a cut that I couldn't even recall Krissi's name last night. "My blood father. My stepmother. They died. They're all dead."

"You didn't know them," Jack said. "They mean nothing to you, Willa."

"Don't tell me what means nothing!" I shouted. "You don't know. You just ask me to pretend all the time. Well, I won't. I'm through pretending. They were my family. They're part of me."

"Willa, this is very hard on all of us," Jack said. "We're trying to make it as easy for you and Terri as possible."

"I don't want it to be easy," I said. "I'm going to Pryor. I'm going to their funeral."

I must have spoken louder than I realized, because Mom came out of the bedroom. She looked like the ghost of the Mom I loved.

"No," she said. "You can't go. I won't let you."

"I have sisters," I said. "Sisters who died. I have to go to their funeral."

"You never knew them," Mom said. "They're strangers, Willa."

"And whose fault is that?" I asked. "Who kept me from them?"

"Willa, that's not fair," Jack said. "Your mother was protecting you. You've got to see that now, see what he really was like."

"He was a killer," I said. "And I'm half his. That's not going to change, not ever, Jack. You think I don't know that?"

"What we all think is that you're overwrought," Curt said. "The past couple of days have been a nightmare for you, for all of you. Maybe Tuesday is too soon for you to go back to school. Maybe you should stay out a few extra days."

"I'll be in Pryor on Tuesday," I said. "I'll stay there until the funerals. By then, everything should be back to normal here. Brooke and Alyssa'll be back home, Jack'll be back at work. We'll act like this never happened." My mind flashed to my little basement refuge. Razors. Cuts. Blood. Release.

"You don't even know where Pryor is," Mom said. "You couldn't find it on a map. And how do you think you'll pay for this trip? You're not getting the money from us."

"I'm not asking you for it," I said. "I have some money saved up. If I have to, I'll borrow from my friends."

"I'll take you," Pauline said. "We'll fly down together. I'll pay."

"Pauline," Curt said.

"Terri, I know you want what's best for Willa," Pauline said. "We all do. But I see things differently from the rest of you. My father died in the war when I was just a baby. Everybody told me about him, what a hero he was. But there's a part of me that's missing, even now, seventy years later, because I didn't get to know the man, the real man. All I knew was the hero, and now all Willa knows is the demon." She paused for a moment, then reached out her hand and touched Jack. "I know you love Willa," she said, "but you have to accept that she isn't your daughter. And Terri, I know you ran away from Dwayne, from Pryor, and that took great courage. But Willa needs to see where she came from. Please, this time, put Willa's needs first."

Mom's face contorted. "All I wanted was to get you away from there," she said to me. "And now you say you have to go back?"

"You got me away," I said. "I'm alive because you got me away. Let me say goodbye to my sisters. They didn't have you. They didn't get away."

I've seen Mom cry before. I've seen her cry at sappy movies on TV, and I've seen her cry tears of pride for me, for Brooke, for Alyssa. I saw her cry on her tenth anniversary, when Jack gave her the diamond ring he couldn't afford before they got married. I saw her cry when she told me her parents had died in a car crash.

I wanted to comfort her, but I couldn't. If she looked at me, she wouldn't see me. She'd see Dwayne and Pryor and everything she'd tried so hard to forget.

"If you want, I can stay with Willa," Pauline said to Jack.

"No," I said. "No, please, Pauline. I can't worry about you while I'm there. Faye'll look after me."

"Well, I'll travel with you," Pauline said. "After you're settled in, I'll go to Santa Fe. I have friends there I haven't seen in a long time. When you're ready to go home, I'll come get you."

"Are you sure?" Jack asked. "It's a big imposition."

"I'm sure," Pauline said. "Curt and I are going to go home now, and the three of you can figure things out. I'll find the best route to Pryor and make the arrangements. We can go tomorrow. Jack, if you call the police, you can tell them I'll be stopping at your house to pack some things for the trip."

"Thank you," I said.

"There are four people in this room who love you, Willa," Pauline said. "Don't you ever forget that."

"I won't," I said, because I knew that was what I was supposed to say. And the Willa Coffey who had existed until two days ago always said and did what she was supposed to.

part two
[pryor]

ten

FAYE OPENED THE DOOR and folded me in her arms. I stood there, shaking uncontrollably, half laughing, half crying, swallowed by her embrace, and feeling, finally, that I was home.

Pauline gave me enough time to pull myself together, and then she introduced herself. Faye knew Pauline would be bringing me, and for a moment I thought she'd hug her as well, but instead she held her hand out, and the two women shook hands and exchanged looks.

I love Willa, each one said with her eyes, and once they both knew it, their smiles became genuine and affectionate.

"I forgot to ask if you're allergic to cats," Faye said as she helped us carry our bags in. "I sure hope you're not, because I've got three of them."

We shook our heads.

"Good," Faye said. "Larry spends most of his time outside, and Curly spends most of his time upstairs, but Moe is a people-person kind of a cat."

A large orange cat proved Faye's point by ramming his head into my ankle. I bent down and patted his head and was rewarded with a purr. It was the sweetest sound I'd heard in days.

"How was the trip?" Faye asked, leading us to her living room. "Are you hungry? I have a snack prepared in case. Would you like something to drink? Tea? Beer? Soda?"

"A beer sounds wonderful," Pauline said.

"My kind of woman," Faye said. "Some ginger ale for you, sweetie?"

"That would be great," I said.

Faye went into her kitchen and came back with two bottles of beer and one of ginger ale. "Sit down," she instructed us. "Anyplace Moe lets you."

We took seats. Moe checked us all out and settled for Faye's lap.

"He knows who feeds him," Faye said, rubbing his head affectionately. "You were saying how the trip was."

"Long," Pauline said. "But we made all our connections and the rental car was waiting for us, so we can't complain."

"I don't see why not," Faye said. "I complain about most anything. Never occurred to me you need a reason."

Pauline laughed. "This may be the best beer I've ever had," she said. "But two more swallows and I'm going to be out."

Faye nodded. "Your bodies are telling you it's an hour later than the clock," she said. "Willa, sweetie, I've got the spare room all set for you. And Pauline, you get my bedroom for the night."

"Oh, I don't want to put you out," Pauline said. "I could stay in a motel."

"There're no empty motel rooms for thirty miles," Faye said. "The reporters are like vultures."

I worried that Pauline would be offended, but instead she laughed. "I'm an old retired reporter myself," she said. "And we certainly can be vultures. But I still don't want to put you out of your bedroom."

"You're not," Faye said. "I sleep on the living room couch most nights anyway."

"I should call Mom," I said. "I told her I'd call when we got here."

"Why don't I show you your room?" Faye suggested. "You can call from there."

I followed Faye upstairs. It wasn't until I saw the twin

bed, carefully made up with pillows and an old patchwork quilt, that I realized just how tired I was.

"This is my grandma's house," Faye said. "Everything got left here, including me. I dug through the attic this morning and found those old yearbooks. I thought you might like looking through them, so I left them on the night table."

"Thank you," I said. "Are there pictures of Mom in there?"

Faye nodded. "And of Budge," she said. "He was in my sister's class in school, so I have those yearbooks too."

I had a thousand questions, but I knew I was too tired to hear any of the answers. "Thank you, Faye," I said. "For letting me stay here. For everything."

Faye hugged me again. "Call Terri and get some sleep," she said. "The bathroom's down the hall, and I left the nightlight on. Don't be surprised if Curly ends up on the bed with you. He's probably in the closet right now. He thinks this is his room."

"I'll like it if he does," I said. "Thanks again, Faye. I'll see you in the morning."

Faye gave me a long look, but then she kissed me good night and left me alone. I called Mom's cell and I got her voice mail, so I called Jack.

"Terri's sleeping," he told me.

I'd spoken to Mom while Pauline was doing the paperwork for the rental car in Amarillo. Still, it seemed odd that she hadn't stayed up for another couple of hours to make sure I'd arrived at Faye's. Either she was still angry at me for my trip to Pryor or the sedatives she was taking had kicked in.

"I'll talk to her tomorrow," I said.

"You could come home tomorrow," Jack said. "And talk to her in person."

"My sisters died," I said. "I'm staying for their funeral."

"Your sisters live in your home," Jack said. "Here in Westbridge. I want to make sure you understand that, pumpkin. We're your family—your mother, Brooke, Alyssa, me. Nothing is ever going to change that."

We both knew everything had changed and we both knew I wasn't supposed to say so. "I'll talk to you tomorrow," I said. "Love you, Jack."

"Love you right back," he said, the way he had for all the life I could remember.

I hung up, used the bathroom, and climbed into bed. A large gray cat jumped onto the foot of the bed, so I shifted over to give him some space.

There was a table lamp next to the bed, and a pile of old high school yearbooks. The most recent one, almost twenty years old, was on top. Pryor High School had a graduating class of forty-two seniors that year, so it was easy enough to find Mom's picture.

It was a formal yearbook picture, and Mom looked subdued, unsmiling. Her hair was long and straight and her gaze seemed to focus outside the frame of the picture, as though she was staring at something far away. Her future maybe, or any place that wasn't Pryor.

It was fascinating to look at Mom's picture, see her as she was when she was just a year older than me. But I was even more intrigued by the quote under her picture.

Don't look for me here, it said. *It's there you'll find me.*

"I'm not looking for you," I whispered as I put the yearbook down. "I'm looking for me, Mom, and I have to look here."

eleven

THE CLOCK BY THE BED said 5:25, but my body told me it was 6:25 and time to get up. Curly was on Texas time and snored gently by my side.

I turned on the lamp and pulled out the oldest of the yearbooks. It took a long time before I found a shot of Budge, but there he was on the football team.

That was the only picture of him from his freshman year, and he had a helmet on, so I couldn't really see him. I pulled out the next year's yearbook and looked some more. He was back on the football team, but he'd made the basketball team as well, so I had a chance to see his face, his body.

He looked like the other boys in the yearbook, grimy and uneasy. I jumped ahead to his senior year and found his formal picture.

Dwayne "Budge" Coffey

They listed his sports teams, but there was no quote. Maybe they didn't have quotes that year, or maybe Budge wasn't the quotable kind. Instead there was a brief description of him:

Budge is one of the most popular boys in school, especially with the girls.

I stared at the picture, trying to see why he was so popular. A quick survey of the other boys showed Budge was one of the better-looking ones, but he wasn't stand-out handsome. There were at least two other boys in his class who I thought were better-looking.

He'd stared sullenly into the lens, looking straight at it, not like Mom with her faraway glance. His downturned mouth, so similar to mine, gave no indication that he even knew how to smile.

But there was something about his eyes, a little narrowed, a little untrusting, that reached out to me, his daughter who hardly remembered him.

If I didn't know him, if I didn't know what had become

of him, would I have stared into those eyes and thought about the pain they could inflict? Would I have said, "Those are the eyes of a killer," or would I simply have thought he was squinting, uncomfortable posing for the picture?

If I hadn't known he was my father, would I have looked at the picture and seen myself in it?

Jack had kept his yearbooks, and Brooke, Alyssa, and I had looked at them once or twice, giggling at the dated clothes and hairstyles. Jack had told us stories about his high school, and he even had a couple of his trophies on display in the den. I knew more about his past than I did my mother's, and until a few days ago, the only thing I'd known about Dwayne Coffey was his name. And even that wasn't accurate, since he went by Budge.

I went back to Mom's yearbook and looked up Faye. She'd gained fifty pounds over the years, but there was still the same kindness in her eyes.

Mom had held on to the one good thing about Pryor, I thought, putting the yearbooks back on the nightstand and preparing myself for what the day might bring.

twelve

PAULINE AND FAYE were sitting at the kitchen table, sipping their coffees. They looked like they'd known each other for years.

"There's orange juice if you want," Faye said. "I'm not a big breakfast person, but there's sweet rolls in the freezer and bread in the fridge for toast, and strawberry jam. I have eggs if you want me to make you some."

"Toast sounds fine," I said. I opened the refrigerator and pulled a couple of slices of white bread out of the package, then dropped them into the toaster. Faye showed me where the plates and glasses were, and I poured myself some orange juice.

"I thought about making you some big fancy breakfast," Faye said. "But that's for company, not family."

"This is fine," I said. "I'm not big on breakfast either."

"We all should be ashamed of ourselves," Pauline said. "Breakfast is the most important meal of the day, and it sounds like none of us eats it."

"If God wanted me to eat a big breakfast, he would have made the day twenty-six hours," Faye said.

We laughed. It felt so strange to hear laughter, like hearing a song you knew sung in a foreign language.

"We were discussing your plans for the day," Pauline said. "Faye's arranged for you to see a lawyer."

"It wasn't much of an arrangement," Faye said. "Sam Whalen's my boss and I schedule his appointments. I cleared a space for us this morning, figured we'd get that over and done with first thing."

"Why do I need to see a lawyer?" I asked. "No one's accused me of anything."

"No, of course not," Faye said. "Besides, Sam's not that kind of a lawyer. Oh, he helps folks with their DUIs, drunk-and-disorderlies, but he's more your everyday kind of lawyer. Wills, real estate, divorces."

"Is he the only lawyer in town?" Pauline asked, helping herself to another cup of coffee.

"There's always two lawyers in any town," Faye said. "No point being a lawyer if you don't have another one to argue with. But Sam's the best, and what he doesn't know, he knows how to find out."

"I still don't see why I need a lawyer," I said, pulling the toast out and spreading jam on it. "I was hoping to do things today. I want to go to the cemetery where Mom's parents are. Maybe meet my great-grandmother, the one that raised Budge."

"Oh, sweetie," Faye said. "You can't go knocking on Mavis Coffey's door and introducing yourself. Her grandson just died and her three great-grandbabies. The last thing she needs is another shock, even if it's the good kind of shock."

"Besides," Pauline said, "Faye has to work, and you have no way to get around."

"So I see this lawyer and then what?" I asked.

"Willa," Pauline said sharply.

"I'm sorry," I said. "I just . . . well, I don't know what I thought, but this is so important to me. Being here and seeing things and learning about my families. Mom won't talk about anything. I guess I wasn't thinking. I guess I don't belong here any more than I belong back home."

"Stop feeling sorry for yourself," Faye said. "It isn't becoming. And start facing reality. This town right now, it's radioactive. I'm not saying everybody here dies peacefully of old age, but we're not used to little children being slaughtered and we're not used to reporters showing up on our doorstep, asking all kinds of questions that make us feel like it's our fault Budge Coffey went crazy. Now Pauline's gone way out of her way to bring you here and I'm taking time off from work, and Sam's rearranged his calendar so he can see you, and we don't expect much from you in return except a little politeness. You think you can do that for us?"

"I'm sorry," I said, feeling my cheeks blush with embarrassment. "I mean it. I really am. Please forgive me."

Faye shook her head. "Willa, sweetie, we all love you and we want to help you get through all this, but you're not the only one suffering around here. Mavis Coffey may be a mean old witch, but even she doesn't deserve this kind of pain, and you may not know Crystal's family, but I do, and they're good, decent folk. Everyone in town is grieving for them. We knew those sweet little girls Budge slashed to death, and he killed us a little bit along with them. So stop dreaming about family reunions and people showing you the love. I'll show you plenty because I've known you since before you were born and your momma is closer to me than my own sister, but to everyone else, you're Budge Coffey's daughter. The lucky one. The one that got away."

"Look," Pauline said, "I don't have to go to Santa Fe. I'll stick around here for the week, if it's all right with you, Faye. The sofa will suit me fine, and then Willa will have company while you're working."

"No," I said. "Pauline, you should see your friends for a few days. And, Faye, you're right, and I really am sorry. I haven't been thinking about anyone but me. I'll see the lawyer, and then I'll do some schoolwork. I brought stuff with me, and it'd be a mistake for me to fall too far behind."

"Good," Faye said. "That's settled. Now eat your toast and get dressed, and we'll go to Sam's and see what's what."

thirteen

"SAM, THIS IS MY GODDAUGHTER," Faye said an hour later, "Willa Coffey. And this is her friend Pauline Henderson, who came with her from Pennsylvania. Willa, Pauline, this is Sam Whalen, the best lawyer in Maynard County."

"She has to say that," Sam said. "I sign her paycheck."

"It's true anyway," Faye said. "I wouldn't be bringing Willa to you if it wasn't."

Sam gestured for us to sit down. I took the chair opposite him, and Pauline and Faye sat on either side of me.

"It's very nice of you to see me," I said. "Faye thinks it's a good idea for me to have a lawyer."

"Everyone should have a lawyer," Sam said. "Otherwise we lawyers would go out of business."

We all laughed, but it wasn't like this morning. It was a polite laughter.

"Faye's told me a bit about your situation," Sam said. "And of course, I know some of the rest. Your momma married a man named McDougal when you were a little girl, but he never adopted you. That right?"

"He would have if he could," I said, "but . . ." And suddenly I didn't know what to call him. Dwayne? Budge? My father? "He couldn't," I finished. "I feel like Jack's my father, though."

Sam nodded. "You're a lucky girl that way," he said. "But as far as the government's concerned, you're Dwayne Coffey's daughter, for better or worse."

"What does that mean, exactly?" Pauline asked.

"Well, for one thing it means Willa's entitled to Social Security benefits," Sam said. "Assuming Dwayne held on to a taxpaying job long enough to put in to the system."

"He worked at the tannery," Faye said. "On and off since high school, and steady since he got sober and found God. That would have been six, seven years by now."

"Well, it won't be much," Sam said. "But Willa's entitled to whatever the benefits are."

"What about Trace?" I asked. "Will I be sharing with him?"

"Trace's Dwayne's boy," Faye said. "Dwayne never married his momma, if that makes any difference."

"No difference at all," Sam said, "as long as Dwayne is listed on the birth certificate as his father. Is he older than Willa or younger?"

"Older," Faye said. "He must be eighteen by now."

"Then he's probably too old for the benefits," Sam said. "Eighteen's the cutoff unless you're still in high school. Now, you'll need your birth certificate. Did you bring yours with you?"

I shook my head. "My mother must have it," I said.

"If she doesn't, she can certainly get a copy," Sam said. "We'll need Dwayne's death certificate also." He wrote something down on a piece of paper.

"Should I be asking for the Social Security?" I asked. "I mean, I didn't know him. Dwayne. I haven't seen him since I was four."

"You're entitled to it," Sam said. "As long as Dwayne paid in to the system. No reason to turn down money the government owes you."

"When the adoption goes through, the Social Security will stop, right?" Pauline asked.

Sam nodded. "So Jack might want to hold off until Willa's eighteen," he said. "Or graduates high school. It's waited this long, it could wait a couple more years."

"I'm not sure Jack will see it that way," Pauline said. "But it is something to consider."

"Now, I don't know if Dwayne left a will," Sam said. "He wasn't my client, but I'll ask around. If he did and he left everything to his wife, then most likely what there is will be divided equally between Willa and Trace."

"There couldn't be that much," Faye said. "He and Crystal had a cute little house, but the bank probably owns more of it than they did."

"Was Dwayne a veteran?" Sam asked.

Faye shook her head.

Sam wrote *veteran* on his pad and crossed it out. "That way I'll remember not to look into it," he said. "Social Security'll make a payment for funeral expenses. Do you know who's going to be making the arrangements?"

"Most likely Mavis Coffey," Faye said. "But you know, the way Budge died, I don't think she'll be making much of a fuss."

"I don't want his money," I said. "Maybe Trace could get it."

"It's going to be more headaches than money anyway," Sam said. "First his debts'll have to be paid off. The house.

The car. The charge cards. We need to check if the house is still officially a crime scene. If Willa can get in, she might want to take a memento or two."

"There's nothing I want," I said.

"We should still make an inventory," Sam said. "Crystal might have left behind some trinkets."

"I don't understand," Pauline said. "Wouldn't Crystal's things go to her family?"

"Depends on her will," Sam said. "Assuming she made one, and it won't surprise me if she didn't. But if she left everything to her little girls, or if she never got around to making a will, then as long as one of those little girls survived her, that child inherited whatever there is. If the court determines Krissi was the last in her family to die, she'd be regarded as Crystal's heir and Willa and Trace would then inherit from her."

"Have you seen an autopsy report?" Pauline asked. "Do they know for sure that Krissi was alive when Dwayne left Pryor?"

Sam shook his head. "I'm going by what I saw on TV," he said. "If the autopsy's been released, I haven't heard about it." He wrote another note.

"What are you saying?" I asked. "If Krissi was still alive when Budge left, then Trace and I inherit Crystal's things?"

Sam nodded. "It goes from Crystal to her daughters, and from her daughters to you and Trace," he said. "Unless

Crystal made a will leaving everything to someone else, her parents or her sisters and brothers. For that matter, we should check to see if the little girls had anything. Sometimes people give babies bonds or a little bit of money. That'd go directly to you and Trace, since there's no will involved."

"That's sick," I said. "My father killed them. Crystal and the girls. I never once laid my eyes on them and my father stabbed them to death, and I'm supposed to take their jewelry and their savings accounts?"

"There's no difference between your taking them and Trace," Sam said.

"It *is* different," I said. "Trace knew them. They're nothing to me. I didn't even know they existed until I heard they were dead. How can I possibly be entitled to their things?"

"It's the law," Sam said. "Same as Social Security. The law's there so we know what the rules are. Without rules, we'd run around fighting each other, not caring what anybody thinks. Sometimes rules can seem arbitrary, and sometimes unfair, but they give us our boundaries, and we need to respect them."

"My father didn't follow the rules," I said. "He was a monster. He broke all the rules. He killed his children. There's blood everywhere because of him. How can the rules be right if, thanks to him, I get money or jewelry or anything?"

"It isn't a question of right and wrong," Sam said. "Of course what Dwayne did was wrong. And if you and your mother decide you shouldn't take anything, then you can refuse your inheritance and it can all go to Trace. But I'd be remiss as a lawyer if I didn't tell you what your rights are. And as your lawyer, I'm going to make sure to find out what there is to inherit, and that it goes to you, for you to decide what to do with. Once you know what there is, what you're legally entitled to, you can decide whether to give your share to Trace or to Crystal's parents or to anybody else you want. But the rules have to be followed, Willa. That's just the way it is."

"Is there anything else?" Pauline asked.

"With all those reporters around, someone might want to talk to Willa," Sam said. "Maybe even make her an offer for her story."

"Her parents would never approve of that," Pauline said. "Never."

"Willa, do you feel the same way?" Sam asked.

"There's nothing I could tell," I said. "I'm here for my sisters' funerals. I don't know anything about Dwayne, about any of them."

"If any reporters come sniffing, we'll send them to you," Faye said. "And you can tell them to go to hell for us."

Sam grinned. "That's one of the things lawyers do best," he said. "All right, Willa. You'll ask your mother about your birth certificate and I'll see what I can do about getting copies of Dwayne's death certificate, and find out if they've determined when Krissi died, and if Dwayne or Crystal made out wills. Do you have any questions?"

"Did you know him?" I asked. "Dwayne. I was wondering if you'd ever met him."

"There are three ways people know each other in this town," Sam said. "School, church, and bars. Dwayne was pretty well known in all those places, so yeah, I knew him, like I know a lot of people around here. I knew Crystal too. I went to school with her mother. There's nobody here who isn't grieving, Willa. But none of that is your fault. Dwayne had his reasons. God had His. You're here because you need to be here, to pay tribute to those sweet little sisters you never had the chance to know. Trust me to do what I do best, looking out for the interests of my clients. Faye here will see to it that I do my job, so you'll have one less thing to deal with. All right?"

"All right," I said, rising from the chair. "And thank you. I know I'm driving everyone crazy. I don't seem to be able to stop myself. Back home—well, I'm a different person back home. Quiet. Nice, I think. But the past few days, I feel like I don't know who I am anymore. So I keep saying the wrong thing and doing the wrong thing, and I can't help it. I'm really sorry."

"You have nothing to apologize for," Sam said. "Not to me, at any rate. Just trust me to do my job. Deal?"

"Deal," I said. "And thank you."

fourteen

Pauline left after we got back to Faye's. She offered to stay until after lunch, but she had a long drive ahead of her and I told her to go.

Then I urged Faye to go back to her office. "I'll be fine," I said. "I ought to call home and start on my homework."

"I'll call you later," Faye said. "And don't be shy about calling me."

"I won't. I promise," I said.

Moe gave Faye a nudge as she left. I went up to my room and, while I sat on the bed, Curly emerged from the closet to keep me company.

I stared at the yearbook pictures of my mother and Budge. I stared at my textbooks. I stared at the quilt, at Curly on the quilt.

Finally I pulled out my cell phone and called home. There was no answer, so I called Mom's cell, but she didn't answer that either.

I felt the now familiar wave of panic wash over me. Somehow, somewhere, my whole family had vanished and I was left alone in Pryor. It was my punishment for being defiant. If I couldn't be Quiet-Never-Make-A-Fuss Willa, Mom and Jack, Brooke and Alyssa, wanted no part of me.

I couldn't even blame them. Quiet-Never-Make-A-Fuss Willa was gone, replaced by the self-pitying, scene-making daughter of a . . .

I couldn't bring myself to define Budge, to put a label on him. Because whatever he was, I was his daughter, and whether I loved him or not, whether I even knew him or not, he was a part of me, so entwined with my body and my soul that he could never be disentangled.

If Jack had been able to adopt me, would I be sitting on this bed, staring at Dwayne Coffey's high school picture? If I'd had as much right as Brooke and Alyssa to call Jack Daddy, would I have truly believed he loved me as much as he loved them?

We're a happy family, I said to myself, closing the year-book and piling it on top of the others. *We have to be.* Because if I didn't have that to believe in, then I had nothing left at all.

fifteen

My cell rang. I answered it. It was Mom, I told myself, or maybe Jack.

But it was Faye. "How're you doing?" she asked. "Hard at work?"

I'd spent so much of my life claiming things were fine when they weren't that it surprised me to hear the truth come from my mouth. "No," I said. "I haven't even tried."

Faye laughed. "At least you're honest about it," she said. "I have a couple of things to tell you. First off, you don't have to worry about the house and the bank and mortgages. Turns out Budge and Crystal rented. I had a nice talk with Harry

Norris—he owns the house—and he said the police are all through with it, and since the rent's paid up till the end of the month, you have plenty of time to go there, look through the things, and make up your mind about what you might want. He said the police did a pretty good job cleaning up, but you can tell something awful happened, so you should be prepared."

"I don't want any of their things," I said.

"Still, you should go through it," Faye said. "Budge's grandma will probably track Trace down so he can get his share, but you're here, so you might as well take what you want. Harry's going to drop the key off later and you can go over tomorrow."

"All right," I said, and Polite Willa kicked in. "Thank you."

"You mentioned wanting to go to your grandparents' grave," Faye said. "I can't get away from the office, so I asked Erma Jenkins to take you. She was good friends with your grandma and grandpa. She knows right where their graves are, so you won't get lost. She'll be dropping by in a few minutes to get you."

"That's very nice of her," I said.

"Well, she's kind of curious about you," Faye said. "Because of your momma, and Erma being friends with the family for so long. I told her you're the quiet type and upset about things so she shouldn't plague you with questions. She said she understood and she thought it was right Christian of you to want to visit your grandparents' graves. The two of you should hit it off just fine."

"Did she know Budge?" I asked.

I could hear Faye sigh. "Honey, this is a small town," she said. "Everybody knows everybody one way or another. If you want to know if she *liked* Budge, well, that's a whole other thing, and you'll have to ask her yourself. Not that anybody's about to say they did."

"No," I said. "Of course not."

"I got an e-mail from your momma," Faye said. "She and Jack are flying down to Orlando for a couple of days. They'll bring the girls back home on Wednesday. Jack thought it would be a good idea for Terri to be out of town until things cool off. She said she'd call you after she and Jack get settled in to a motel."

I pictured Mom alone in the motel while Jack had dinner with Val and their daughters. It didn't matter. She'd probably be so knocked out by sedatives, she wouldn't notice.

"I'd better get back to work," Faye said. "Sam's still digging around, trying to find out what's rightfully yours. Now you be nice to Erma and I'll be home around five to hear all about it."

I said goodbye and hung up. My family really had vanished. I couldn't imagine a time before when Mom and Jack might have taken off for some place, any place, without letting me know first.

"Well, I hope they'll all be happy in Orlando," I muttered. I pictured them in a Sears photograph, Jack with his wives on either side, Brooke, Alyssa, and Mickey Mouse seated in front of them.

I laughed. Curly gave me a look and that made me laugh even harder.

"I'll never replace you with a mouse," I said. "Not even Mickey."

That must have satisfied him, because he yawned and went back to sleep. I would have done the same except I was too nervous about meeting Erma Jenkins. So I went downstairs and sat at the front window, waiting for her to arrive.

She did about ten minutes later. She rang the bell and I opened the door. As I did a cat scurried in. Larry, I guessed, the mostly outdoors cat.

"You must be Willa," the woman said. "Terri Doreen's little girl."

"I am," I said. "Are you Mrs. Jenkins?"

"That I am," she said, looking me over carefully. "You're all Coffey, aren't you," she said. "I don't see a bit of Penders in you."

I've always known I don't look like my mother, but

Mom would never admit it. Jack likes to say he can see Mom in my smile or in some small gesture.

Mrs. Jenkins checked me out some more. "All Coffey," she said. "But I suppose that's not your fault. You ready to go?"

"Yes," I said, grabbing my bag. "Is the cemetery far?"

"We'll drive it, if that's what you mean," Mrs. Jenkins said. "I know how you city folk can't stand walking."

There was no point explaining that I didn't live in a city. Instead I allowed myself to look at Mrs. Jenkins, although not as boldly as she'd looked at me.

She was old, older even than Pauline, and she was thin, with short, no-nonsense hair and dried-out skin. I might be all Coffey, but Mrs. Jenkins looked all Pryor to me, the kind of person Mom had been so desperate to escape from, even in high school.

"How's Terri Doreen?" she asked as she floored the gas pedal, paying no attention to the stop sign at the corner.

"She's fine," I said. "Did you know her when she was growing up?"

"Of course I did," Mrs. Jenkins said, barely swerving to avoid a woman dragging a screaming toddler across the street. "I was at her christening. What a day that was. After all poor Clara had been through, you'd have thought the crown princess had been born."

"Clara?" I said.

"Your grandmother," Mrs. Jenkins said. "Your momma never bothered telling you your grandparents' names?"

"No, of course she did," I said. "Clara and Doyle Penders. I just never think of them that way." *Or any way at all,* I thought. "What had she been through?"

"All those poor babies," Mrs. Jenkins said. "Well, you'll see soon enough."

The way she was driving, I figured we'd end up in the cemetery right alongside my grandparents. And even with her speeding, it took ten minutes to get there. Definitely too long a walk for us city folk.

I tried to remember the last time I'd been to a cemetery, but the funny thing was, I couldn't be sure I'd ever been to one. I'd attended a couple of funerals, one for Jack's great-uncle, another for the mother of one of my friends. But I hadn't gone to the cemetery for the actual burial either time. So I wasn't sure what to expect, except that Pryor seemed such a dirt-poor town from the little I'd seen of it, and I thought the cemetery would have the same dusty, worn-out look.

But I guess the people of Pryor spent their money on keeping their cemetery nice. There were trees there, and lots of bouquets by gravesites, and the tombstones varied in size and fanciness.

"Should I have brought flowers?" I asked Mrs. Jenkins as she drove through.

"I got you some," she said. "On the floor in the back."

I turned around and saw a supermarket bouquet. "Thank you," I said.

"Had to go to Center City to get them," she replied. "Every flower in town's already been bought for poor Crystal and the babies."

"I really appreciate it," I said. "And thank you for bringing me here."

"Doyle and Clara were my friends," Mrs. Jenkins said. "Damn shame the way their children treated them." She braked so hard, I thought the airbags would inflate. "The Penders family plot is over there," she said. "Get the flowers and you can see."

I unbuckled the seat belt, got out of the car, and then opened the back door and reached over to get the flowers. I wasn't sure if I should offer to pay for them, but it seemed wrong to ask at the cemetery.

Instead I followed Mrs. Jenkins to the Penders plot. All their tombstones were small and unadorned, although other graves nearby had angels and crosses.

"The Penders were never much for fancy displays," Mrs. Jenkins said. "Good thing too, since Martin wasn't going to shell out for anything fancy. Practically a crime, the coffins he put his parents in."

"I think things look nice," I said, walking over and inspecting the various names. Some of the dates were from the 1880s.

"Your great-great-grandparents," Mrs. Jenkins said. "Or great-great-greats. I lose track. But there've been Penders in Pryor as long as there's been a town."

I had never really thought of myself as a Penders. My last name was Coffey and Mom's was McDougal. It was a strange sensation to be standing there surrounded by the remains of family I had never known, would never know.

"Martin must not have much money," I said, bending over to read names and dates. "He has such a big family."

Mrs. Jenkins snorted. "He was mad, that's all. Had no right to be, with Terri Doreen cut out of the will altogether."

"Why was she cut out?" I asked.

"For stealing," Mrs. Jenkins said. "Taking money from Doyle's wallet so she could run out on her husband. Not that he approved of that either. Doyle always took marriage vows real serious."

"Mom was desperate," I said. "She had to get out." I remembered her yearbook. Most likely, she'd been looking for an excuse. Just as likely, Budge provided her with plenty.

"There they are," Mrs. Jenkins said, pointing to one larger tombstone and a row of small ones.

The large one said DOYLE PENDERS / CLARA PENDERS, with the years of their birth and death. Martin really hadn't gone for a lot of frills.

I put the flowers down and looked at the small ones. Two said BABY BOY PENDERS and two said BABY GIRL PENDERS.

"Stillborns," Mrs. Jenkins said. "One before Martin and three more before Terri Doreen."

I gasped. "Did Mom know?" I asked.

"Of course she did," Mrs. Jenkins said. "We respect our dead in Pryor. Martin and Terri Doreen came to the cemetery regular with Doyle and Clara."

Budge had five children, I thought. Martin had eight. My grandparents six. Mom had one. Had Brooke and Alyssa and I kept her and Jack from having more? If you asked her, she'd say she has three daughters.

"You said Martin was mad," I said, straightening up and looking around at all the family I would never know. "What was he mad about?"

"Not getting any of the insurance money," Mrs. Jenkins said. "Not that he would have spent it on fancy tombstones. Just given it to that strange cult he belongs to."

"Why didn't he get insurance money?" I asked. "They died in a car crash, right? I thought accidents were covered by insurance."

"Doyle's blood alcohol level was too high for the insurance people," Mrs. Jenkins said.

"He was drunk?" I said. "He was driving drunk?"

"There's a difference between one beer too many and drunk," Mrs. Jenkins said. "It was Saturday night, he'd put in a long week at the tannery, and he and Clara went out with some friends. Doyle liked his beer. Most folks around here do, even those who pretend they don't and try to keep others from drinking. Don't know where they get that idea. Plenty of drinking in the Good Book."

"Mom didn't go to the funeral," I said. "I thought it was because I was too young, or she and Jack couldn't afford to go."

"People here said it was because she was too ashamed to show her face," Mrs. Jenkins said. "Stealing from her daddy and running away like that. And some said she knew she'd been cut out of the will and that was why. But I figured she was just too damn mad. She loved her momma so, and Clara worshiped the ground she walked on. No love lost between Terri Doreen and Doyle, though, and then with the sheriff saying the accident was his fault, I don't think Terri Doreen had it in her to forgive him. Probably still hasn't."

She must have been so ashamed, I thought. Jack's parents were such nice people: two kids, five grandkids (not including me), center hall colonial, Irish setter. Not rich like Val's parents, but more the way you imagined grandparents to be. And there was Jack with his college degree, a career he loved, two remarkable daughters, and an ex-wife rapidly rising up the corporate ladder.

Mom had a high-school diploma, a brother in a cult, a violent ex-husband named Budge, and parents who died from drunk driving.

For the first time in days, I felt something other than anger and resentment. I felt sorry for Mom, sorry for where she'd come from and what she didn't have.

"It's so sad," I said, gesturing at the tombstones, at the ones for the four stillborn babies. "So much loss."

"It'll be worse on Wednesday," Mrs. Jenkins said. "When the Coffey babies are laid to rest."

sixteen

Mom called me that night, after Faye and I had eaten what passed for pizza in Pryor. If I'd given any serious thought to staying in Pryor and working at the tannery, the pizza convinced me otherwise.

Faye tactfully moved into the kitchen, taking the dishes and remains with her.

"We're in Orlando," Mom said. "Faye told you?"

"Yeah, this afternoon," I said. "Mom, I went to the cemetery today. I saw where all the Penders are buried."

"Oh," she said. "I didn't think you'd want to do that."

"I did," I said. "Erma Jenkins took me. She said you and your mother were really close, that she worshiped the ground you walked on."

"She was a good woman," Mom said. "She shouldn't have died the way she did."

"I'm sorry," I said. "I wish you'd tell me more about her. I'd like to know."

"After you get back," Mom said. "She loved you so much when you were little. She practically raised you for a while there. I was working, so she looked after you."

"I remember a little bit," I said. "She had a big picture of Jesus. And a cat. And there was a cuckoo clock."

"You loved that clock," Mom said. "That's the one thing Momma and Daddy had that I wanted. I asked Martin if I could have it, but he said no, it was Daddy's express wish I not get anything from them. I told myself it didn't matter, that you'd already forgotten about the clock by then."

"I haven't thought about it in years," I said. "What was the cat's name, do you remember?"

"Ezekiel," Mom said. "Big old tomcat. As ornery as Granny Coffey."

"I wish you were here," I said.

"I'm never going back," Mom said. "I spent half my life trying to escape. I don't even like knowing you're there."

"I know," I said. "I'm sorry. But it felt so important to

me to be here. And I was angry at you. I'm not sure why anymore, just that I was."

"We'll talk about it when we're all home," Mom said. "I love you, Willa. All I want is for you to be safe and happy."

"I know," I said. "How's Orlando? Is Jack with you?"

"He's at Val's," Mom said. "It's a real mess."

"Why?" I asked. "What happened?"

"What didn't?" Mom replied. "The plan was for us to stay at Curt's and Jack to go back to work today. We figured the girls would fly home on Tuesday. But yesterday Brooke had a total meltdown."

"Brooke?" I said. Brooke never goes crazy. It's not that bad things don't happen to her, although they don't very often. But on those rare occasions when she's disappointed or upset, she just shrugs it off. No, worse. She shrugs it off with a smile, a laugh.

"Brooke," Mom said. "I can't blame her. At first she said she was okay with everything that happened, but Sunday afternoon, one of her friends called to say she'd heard that Budge had carried Krissi's head to our door."

"He didn't, did he?" I asked.

"No," Mom said, a little too quickly. "No. People make things up. But that's the story that's making the rounds, and Brooke believed it." She inhaled deeply. "Well, why not believe it?" she said. "It doesn't matter if it's true or not. He was driving around for God knows how long with Krissi's dead body in the back of the car. He slaughtered her, her sisters, her mother. Why not carry her head around like a bowling ball?"

"Mom," I said.

"I'm sorry," she said. "I guess Brooke could handle things when it happened in Pryor, but once it reached our front door, it was too much for her. There was no way she could travel on her own, let alone with Alyssa to look after."

"So Val insisted Jack come get them," I said.

"It was Jack's idea," Mom said. "He figured we'd both be better off away from home until things cooled down. We flew to Orlando this morning."

"Is Brooke better?" I asked. "Would it help if I called?"

"Give her a day or two," Mom said. "Jack's been at Val's since we got here. He called to tell me he'd have supper there, and he said Brooke was still shaky."

"So you're all alone in Orlando," I said.

"Jack'll be here in a little while," Mom said.

"How's Alyssa doing?" I said. "Is she upset also?"

Mom inhaled sharply. "Things are a little complicated there," she said. "Val made an appointment for them to go to the tennis academy tomorrow, really talk about Alyssa's future. Val told Jack . . . well, with Brooke acting up the way she is, Val has it in her head the girls would be better off living with her. Brooke will be in college, but Val wants her during vacations, and Alyssa full-time. Jack would never say it, but I think Val's using the tennis academy to get Alyssa to agree."

"Can Jack stop her?" I asked. "Val, I mean." No one would be able to stop Alyssa.

"I don't know," Mom replied. "With Brooke gone, and Val back, and the tennis academy so close to where Val lives, maybe not. We can't afford a custody battle, and Jack would never do that to Alyssa anyway. But the academy might tell them Alyssa is too young, that she's better off where she is. Or Brooke might convince Alyssa to stay with us. Or Alyssa might decide she's happier with us than she would be at Val's. Val has to travel so much on business. After Munich, it's a month in Hong Kong. She told Jack she'd hire a live-in housekeeper, but that's no way for Alyssa to be raised."

"It sounds pretty bad," I said.

"Jack's upset, naturally," Mom said. "But we'll all be home by the end of the week. And things are bound to get better. I've been afraid for twelve years now, afraid of Budge, what he might do to you, to me. I don't have to be afraid anymore. That's got to make a difference."

"I love you, Mom," I said. "And Jack. I love him too. And I'm sorry."

"I'm sorry too," she said. "But I don't think any of this is our fault."

seventeen

FAYE WOKE ME UP from the first good night's sleep I'd had in days. "I'm sorry, sweetie," she said. "But Sam's going to be in court all day, and he needs me in the office."

"That's okay," I mumbled, still caught up in the final fragments of my dream.

"There's time for you to take a shower and have some breakfast," Faye said. "Then we'll go to the house. I don't want you going there alone, but if you're okay once we get there, I'll go to the office. It's only a few blocks from here, practically a straight line, so you should be fine walking home."

I had no idea what she was talking about. Curly, who'd

woken up long enough to stretch and turn over before falling back asleep, provided no answers.

"What house?" I said.

Faye looked uncomfortable. "Budge and Crystal's," she said. "You need to see if there's anything there you want. Or if there's any loose change lying around. It's as much yours as anybody's."

There was no point telling Faye I wasn't interested. She was, and that was enough.

"Okay," I said. "I'll be downstairs in a few minutes."

"Take your time," Faye said. "Well, don't fall back asleep or anything."

"Fifteen minutes," I said. "I promise."

Faye left me and I left Curly. I was as good as my word and was standing in the kitchen, toasting frozen waffles, a few minutes later. Not a breakfast Mom would approve of. I wondered what Val served the girls for breakfast. I'd have to ask them when we all got home.

Faye kept looking at the kitchen clock, so I ate the waffles and drank the orange juice in record time. "It's real easy from here," she said as I grabbed my bag and a key to her house. "We make a right turn out of the driveway and go for four stop signs, and then make a left onto West Houston. Then five blocks to Maplewood Street, a right at the light, and another two blocks on Johnson. That's where the house is, four twenty-two Johnson Street. I wrote the directions for you, only in reverse, so you can get home. Shouldn't be much more than a fifteen-minute walk."

"It's a nice day for a walk," I said. "It'll feel good to get some exercise."

Faye looked at the clock in the car. "It's been one of those mornings," she said. "Everything would be better if I woke up ten minutes earlier."

"I'm sorry," I said.

"Oh, it's not your fault, honey," she said. "It's just with the funeral tomorrow, Sam and Harry Norris were both concerned Crystal's family might want to go to the house and start taking things that aren't rightfully theirs. I do feel bad about leaving you alone, but it's better if we do things quiet-like. The less fuss, the better."

I don't know what hidden treasure Faye thought might be lying there. "Did Crystal work?" I asked.

"Not after the twins were born," Faye said. "They were preemies and something wasn't right with Kadi, so Crystal stayed home with them."

"And Budge worked at the tannery."

"Most everyone does around here," Faye replied. "If it ever closes shop, Pryor'll close right along with it. All right. See, here's the turn onto Johnson. They put the traffic light up about ten years ago, after a big accident. A pickup plowed into a car with a half dozen high school kids. The mayor's daughter was killed, along with a couple of her cousins. It's like a memorial traffic light."

As we drove to the house, we could see the traffic light wasn't the only memorial. The small yard in front of 422 Johnson was covered with bouquets of flowers, teddy bears, dolls, crosses, and handmade cards signed seemingly by hundreds of people.

"Well, it's to be expected," Faye said. "Don't know why Harry didn't bother to tell me, though."

She pulled the car up in front of the house, and we both got out reluctantly. It felt like a desecration to walk through the offerings, knowing I was going in not out of love or reverence but to take any loose change I might find, or a memento of the strangers who happened to be my closest relatives.

"There might be things that belong to somebody else," I said, hoping that would be a good enough reason for us to turn around and go home. "Something they borrowed from friends or relatives. I wouldn't want to take anything that belongs to someone else."

Faye pulled an envelope out of her bag and handed it to me. I could feel the key inside it. "Take the jewelry," she whispered. "Anything you find like that. Any cash. If you should find bankbooks, or any papers that look important, take those. No one's asking you to take a skillet or the towels."

"You're coming in with me, right?" I asked.

"Just for a second," Faye said. "But you should be the one to unlock the door. Seeing as it's your family, your inheritance."

I hated this. I hated all of it. I knew Jack would never let me go through something like this alone. But I couldn't make a scene. I was the one who'd insisted on coming to Pryor. They were my family, I'd said. Faye had taken me in, done everything she could for me. And according to her, this was what family did.

I unlocked the door.

There was a bad smell to the house, like something rotten had stayed in there too long and windows hadn't been opened, but it wasn't too bad. It wasn't so overwhelming that we had to escape.

But whether I wanted to or not, I could hear the crying, the screaming. I felt enveloped by terror, attacked by rage.

"Where?" I asked.

Faye understood. "Kadi was in bed with Crystal," she replied. "Maybe she hadn't been feeling well. They think Budge went after Crystal first, but he wasn't methodical or anything, and there was blood all over. Crystal must've tried to protect Kadi, but there was nothing she could do. Budge had six inches and forty pounds on her, and a hunting knife.

It's from the way the bodies were they think Crystal tried to save Kadi."

"And the others?" I asked, swallowing hard.

"Kelli Marie was in the bathtub," Faye said. "In her nightie. The police figure she heard what was happening and ran into the bathroom to hide. They don't know where Krissi was, maybe in bed sleeping through it all. The only rooms with a lot of blood were the bedroom and the bath, but Budge must've stepped into some of it, because there were tracks on the floor. He left from the kitchen, carrying Krissi they guess, and drove off."

"Nobody heard?" I asked.

"The TV was on," Faye said. "Everyone keeps their TVs on all the time. Even if the neighbors heard something, they probably thought it was just a show."

"And nobody suspected anything?" I asked. It was inconceivable to me that if Jack and Mom and Brooke and Alyssa and I were all missing, no one would notice.

"Crystal spoke to her momma, but not every day," Faye said. "Her folks both work at the tannery. They don't necessarily feel like conversation after a long day. And it wasn't like this was the only time Budge missed a day at work. The second day he didn't show up, they called here, and when they didn't get an answer, they started calling around." She looked at her watch. "Honey, I got to get going," she said. "Try not to think about what happened. Just go through the things, take what you think is important, and go home. Call me when you get back, all right? And remember, if anybody comes to the door, you have as much right to be here as anybody. More than anybody, seeing as they were your sisters." She gave me a quick peck on the cheek. "I'll see you tonight," she said. "Maybe we'll go to Dairy Queen after supper."

"That'd be nice," I said, because I was supposed to say something.

Faye nodded and walked out, leaving me alone with the jewelry and the loose change and the scent of blood.

My blood, I thought. That's what you call family. Blood relatives.

I looked around at the living room, not knowing what I was supposed to be seeing. It was cluttered with toys, dolls and puzzles and coloring books with crayons strewn around the floor.

I was four when Mom took me away from Budge, the same age as the twins. I must have left toys like these behind.

I didn't remember. I could picture my grandmother's cuckoo clock now, and the painting of Jesus. She'd had a vase with plastic flowers on a table under that painting, and I'd loved the flowers because they always were in bloom. But I didn't remember what my home had looked like, whether it had been littered with crayons and puzzles.

I forced myself to look up, to truly look around the room. Crystal and Budge also had a picture of Jesus on the wall, but theirs was above the TV set. There was a plaid sofa with a couple of cigarette burn holes in it, and I realized some of the unpleasant odor was stale cigarette smoke. Sure enough, on an end table next to a recliner was an ashtray with half a dozen butts in it.

Mom had smoked, I remembered. She'd quit around the time she'd met Jack. Maybe she'd seen that he didn't smoke or maybe she'd had to choose between cigarettes and food. Another question to ask her when we were at a point where we could talk about her life before.

There was a bookshelf on the wall opposite the sofa. It held a few picture books, a handful of paperback romances, a Bible. On the bottom shelf were toy boxes, and on the top were photographs, the Sears one that had been shown end-lessly on the cable news stations, and one of Santa holding Kelli Marie, a second of him holding the twins.

There was another formal photograph, a couple smiling at each other. The wedding picture, I realized. I walked over and picked it up. Crystal had on a light blue dress and was holding a bouquet of pink roses. She looked so young, so full of hope. Budge's smile looked insincere, posed. But maybe he was self-conscious or blinded by the flash. He had on an ill-fitting jacket, with one of the roses as a boutonniere.

There was another picture from the wedding, this one crowded with family. Most of them looked like Crystal, or at least not like Budge. Two of them stood closer to him than to her. One, an old woman squinting and scowling, I recognized right away as Granny Coffey. She'd scared me when I was little, I suddenly remembered. She yanked me by the ear and told me bad little girls went straight to hell, where they burned screaming for their mommies forever and ever. I cried and she said God didn't care if I cried because He didn't love wicked little girls like me.

Another time, I remembered, she chased me out of the house with a broom, locked the door, and left me standing there, no coat on, for what felt like hours. It might have been hours, for all I knew. Mom had found me and carried me into the house and Granny Coffey had said she'd fallen asleep and forgotten all about me. Mom yelled so loud, she scared me almost as much as Granny Coffey had, and that night she and Daddy got into a huge fight. They woke me up, they were so loud and scary, and I watched from the living room doorway as they fought with curse words and fists.

Daddy. He was my daddy then and I'd loved him. Even when I was bad and he paddled me hard, I loved him.

I'll be good, I'd promised him. I'll never do it again.

Mostly he'd stop then and he'd kiss me and say he sure hoped I'd learned my lesson. Once, maybe twice, he didn't stop. It was like he couldn't, and Mommy had to pull me away from him. He'd burst out crying, and it scared me more to see him like that than all the beatings in the world.

Daddy.

I felt assaulted by the memories; they were hitting me as hard as Daddy used to hit me. I shook my head, as though I could knock the thoughts out of it, and forced myself to focus on the boy standing between Budge and Granny Coffey in the wedding picture. He looked to be twelve or thirteen, in a slightly too-tight jacket and slacks that were a little too short, like he'd had a growth spurt too recently to buy new clothes.

He didn't seem to mind, though. Except for Crystal, he was the only person in the picture who seemed genuinely happy. He was a younger, happier version of Budge, and he looked so much like me that I knew he had to be my brother.

I put the picture back. There was nothing else in the living room with any meaning for me. Now that I'd seen the photographs, I would always remember what Budge and Granny Coffey looked like, and what they'd been like to Mom and me.

I went to the kitchen next. It was a small house, probably no more than four rooms. I wasn't ready for the bedrooms yet.

There were unwashed dishes in the sink. A glass half full of soda sat on the table, a couple of dead flies floating in it.

Budge had left through the back door, most likely carrying Krissi. He had to have washed the blood, or most of it, off himself first. He couldn't have cleaned himself in the bathroom, not with Kelli Marie lying there in the tub.

I forced myself to walk to the kitchen sink. There was blood on the dishes, on the faucets, on the walls of the sink. It was week-old blood, and some effort had been made to clean it, but I still could see it.

Why had Faye brought me here? These people had no money, no jewelry. There was nothing of sentimental value for me, and she had to have known there wouldn't be.

It was some form of shock treatment, I thought. I was left alone in this house so I could finally understand what Budge had done. To make sure I realized this wasn't some cable news stranger but my daddy.

It sounded cruel, but I knew it wasn't. Faye was no Granny Coffey. Jack would never have okayed this, but Jack wanted all of us to believe in happy families.

Mom needed me to understand why she'd run away, what she'd been so frightened of for so long. But I still wasn't sure she'd want me in this house, and even if she did, I knew she'd want Faye here by my side.

I couldn't tell her Faye had left me. Faye was the only part of Pryor that Mom still had. Mom would never forgive her for leaving me here alone.

We were a family of secrets. I'd kept my share. One more wouldn't hurt.

There was no reason to stay in the kitchen. Crystal might have been the type to keep a few dollars hidden in the sugar bowl, but I wasn't about to dig around and find out.

The problem was where I would go if I left the kitchen. As best I could tell, the only rooms left were the girls' room, the master bedroom, and the bath.

I knew I couldn't leave without going to Budge and Crystal's bedroom. Faye would be certain to ask me, and she'd catch me if I lied. I could skip the bathroom, I told myself. But I had to go to the bedroom, and if I wanted Faye to shut up about it, I'd better find Crystal's jewelry box and take something from it.

I went to the girls' room first, where no one had died. It was painted pink and had white cotton curtains. Most of the girls' toys seemed to be in the living room, but there were a couple of dolls strewn around here, and a well-chewed teddy bear in the corner.

There were two beds with identical pink flowered sheets and quilts. Kelli Marie must have had her own, and the twins shared another. Neither bed was made.

I looked across the tiny room and saw the remains of bloody fingerprints on the chest of drawers and closet. Budge needed clothes for Krissi. The people who'd seen her in Ohio had described her outfit, blue jeans and a yellow cotton shirt. If she'd been in bed when Budge went on his rampage, he must have dressed her before they left.

It didn't help that I was in the room where no one had died. This bedroom was as filled with ghosts as anywhere else in the house.

I went to the master bedroom.

I knew there'd be blood there, but I hadn't expected quite so much. There was no headboard and the walls were splattered. The mattress had been torn to shreds from Budge's ceaseless stabbing.

I knew I couldn't stay in the room very long. *Just find something, anything,* I told myself, *and then you can go back to Faye's spare room with its patchwork quilt and sleeping cat.*

Bloody footprints covered the carpet. There were pale but discernible bloodstains on the furniture and closet, showing what Budge had touched after he'd washed himself off in the kitchen.

Crystal's jewelry box was on top of the chest of drawers.

I stood as far away as I could, reached out, and grabbed it. As I opened it, the sound of a tinkling music box song shocked me. I screamed and dropped the box, Crystal's earrings and pendants scattering on the carpet.

"Who's there? Whoever you are, you've got no business being here!"

I screamed again.

eighteen

"GET OUT OF THAT room right now! Do you hear me? Get out!"

I couldn't move. The music box kept tinkling "Edelweiss." The footsteps got louder and closer to the door.

"Out! You got no right being here."

I stared, paralyzed with fear, at a young man, not much more than a boy, really, in tight jeans and a white T-shirt, a tattoo of a dragon reaching from his neck all the way down his left arm. In confusion, I thought, Budge didn't have a tattoo, not when he was that age, when my mother loved him enough to make his baby.

Then I understood. "Trace?" I choked out. "You're Trace?"

He looked at me, Budge's daughter, his sister. As much a Coffey as he was.

"Willa?" he asked.

I managed to nod.

"I heard you was in town," he said. "Granny heard talk."

"I didn't know you were," I said. I took a deep breath, trying to stop my body from shaking. "I . . . I'm sorry. I don't want to be here. I haven't taken anything."

"Not much to take, most likely," Trace said. "Except for his guitar. I came to get his guitar."

Everything was swirling. Out of nowhere, I remembered Daddy playing "Itsy Bitsy Spider" on his guitar, teaching me its words, laughing with me as I danced to the music.

"Oh, God," I said. "I'm going to be sick."

"Bathroom," Trace said.

"No," I said. "Not there." I raced through the hallway, the bloodstained kitchen, and out the back door. I made it to the tiny backyard just in time. The swing set swayed almost playfully in the tannery-scented breeze.

Trace followed me out. "You okay?" he asked.

"No," I said. "I mean, yes, I guess so. My heart's stopped pounding."

"Sorry," he said. "I didn't know it was you. Can you go back in? The living room's not bad."

I nodded. We walked down the driveway to the front of the house. Trace opened the door.

"Everybody's watching," he said. "The whole town probably knows by now that we're in here talking."

"I don't care," I said. "I'll be gone in a couple of days."

Trace laughed, and when he did, I heard another of Budge's echoes. "No one stays in Pryor if they don't have to," he said.

"You didn't," I said, sitting on the plaid sofa, the kindly face of Jesus staring down at me.

"Well, I don't know how much of a choice I had," Trace said. He sat on the easy chair, picked up the ashtray, then pushed it away. "Crystal and me had a big fight and Granny wouldn't let me stay with her neither. No one else was much interested, so I took off."

"To where?" I asked.

"Austin first," he said. "Then Memphis. I've been thinking maybe I'd try Nashville next. I could use a good guitar, so I figured I'd help myself to Budge's. You don't want it, do you?"

"I don't want anything," I said. "How did you find out?"

"About Crystal and the girls? I saw it on TV. How about you?"

"Faye Parker called the police," I said. "After Budge took

Krissi. She was worried about Mom and me. Did Budge know where you were?"

Trace shook his head. "No one did," he said. "Crystal made it damn clear she didn't want any part of me, and Budge didn't care one way or the other. The twins were still in the hospital when I left. Kelli Marie used to follow me around, though. She couldn't say Trace. More like Twace." He paused. "I knew you was Willa right away. I could hear Momma Terri in your voice when you said my name."

"You called her that?" I asked. "Momma Terri?"

"Yeah," he said. "I was just a little kid when I lived with you folks. My momma had taken up with some guy—well, she was always doing that, still is probably—and she didn't want me around, so she sent me back to live with Budge and Momma Terri and you."

I tried to picture this, Daddy and Mommy and my big brother, Trace. A happy family, happy in its own fashion.

"What happened?" I asked.

Trace looked up, like he was trying to catch the memory. "I'm not sure," he said. "But my momma got me and I lived with her for a while, and then I lived with some other folks, and then Budge found Jesus and I came back here to live with him and Granny Coffey. I lived with Granny till she kicked me out, and then I lived with Budge and Crystal till she kicked me out, and you know the rest."

"I thought it was the other way around," I said. "Granny kicked you out last."

Trace laughed. It was an easy laugh and hearing it made me feel better. "Could be," he said. "I got kicked out so many times, I coulda lost the order of things. So what's your life been like since I stopped changing your diapers?"

"You changed my diapers?" I asked, trying hard not to blush.

He laughed again. "I don't know how much of a help I was," he said. "But Momma Terri always tried to make me feel like I was. She was real kind to me. Sometimes I'd wish she was my real momma. I'd wish she'd come and find me and we'd live together again, you and Momma Terri and Budge and me. You know. Kid stuff."

"I know," I said, although I really didn't. Had Brooke and Alyssa ever fantasized like that, that Jack and Val would miraculously get back together? I had no memories of wanting Budge back in my life, but then again, until today I'd had no memories of him at all.

And now I was sitting in his living room talking with his son. Swapping stories. Reminiscing. A blood-soaked family reunion.

"My life is pretty good," I said. "No, it's really good. Mom married this great guy. He would've adopted me, but Budge wouldn't let him."

"Sounds like Budge," Trace said. "Never give anything up, if someone else wants it."

"Anyway, I feel like Jack is my father," I said. "He has two daughters, and they live with us. We're happy. I mean, we fight and we don't always get along, but Mom and Jack love us and we love them. And each other." I sounded like an idiot. "I'm a junior in high school," I said. "And I sing in the choir."

"You sing?" Trace asked, and his face lit up. "Me too. Budge had a great voice, really great. He used to say if my momma hadn't had me, and then him meeting up with Momma Terri and all, he would have gone to Nashville to see if he could make it. I bet he could have too. He played a mean guitar. Learned all by himself, and then he taught me. What kind of songs you like to sing?"

I'd never really thought about it. I sang what was assigned. "Just about anything," I said. "I don't know how good I am, but I'm getting a solo in the next recital." Funny. No one in my family knew that yet. Trace was the first I'd told.

"That's real nice," Trace said. "Maybe before you go, we'll sing something together."

"I'd like that," I said. "No one else in my family sings. Does Granny Coffey?"

Trace shook his head. "She sings like a crow." He laughed. "I guess it comes from Great-Grandpa Coffey's side of the family, but he took off way before I was born, so I don't know. Never asked Budge."

"Maybe we could ask Granny Coffey," I said.

"Yeah," Trace said. "But I ain't willing to risk my life trying."

I laughed with him. And then I remembered where I was.

I guess Trace did too, because his laughter stopped almost as abruptly as mine had.

"She's a mean little bitch," he said. "Meanest I ever come across, and I met my share."

"But she's letting you stay with her," I said.

"Sorta," Trace said. "I'm sleeping on the porch. She lets me in to use the john and then she chases me out again. I was thinking I might stay here, but the bedroom's a mess, and I don't think I'd be comfortable in the girls' room. I could sleep on the couch here, though. It'd be warmer than the porch."

"It's a rental," I said. "And the rent's paid up till the end of the month. I don't see why you couldn't stay here. If you can stand it, I mean."

"That's a good question," he said. "I guess I won't know until I try."

I turned away from him. Jesus smiled at me. "The reason I'm here . . ." I began. "Well, I'm in Pryor because I wanted to go to the funeral. They were my sisters, even if I didn't know them. I felt like I should be here."

Trace nodded. "I understand," he said. "I'm here too."

"What I meant was the reason I'm *here,* in their house," I continued. "Faye works for a lawyer, Sam Weldon. I saw him yesterday morning, and he said if Crystal hadn't made out a will or if she did and she left everything to her daughters, then I'd inherit from them. You and I. Since we're their closest relations."

"Wouldn't the money go to Crystal's folks?" Trace asked.

"Not according to Sam," I said. "Not if Krissi was the last one to die. She'd inherit from Crystal, and then we inherit from her. My guess is there isn't very much, the house being a rental and all."

Jesus continued to smile at me.

"How did you get in anyway?" I asked. "Did Granny have a key?"

"I broke in through the kitchen door," Trace said. "When I heard that music box go off, I damn near had a heart attack."

"Me too," I said, laughing with my brother the housebreaker.

"I wouldn't mind inheriting something," Trace said. "If there's anything to inherit. Crystal kind of owes me, you know. Kicking me out like she did. I figured I could take the guitar because I knew it was Budge's, but I didn't know I could take everything else. Half of everything else."

"I didn't see anything worth taking," I said. "Not that I looked very hard."

"Sit here," Trace said. "I'll get that jewelry box. Maybe there's something pretty in there for you." He left the room and I went back to looking at the wedding pictures, staring at Trace without a tattoo.

He returned a few moments later. I could make out the outline of some jewelry in his pockets. "There wasn't hardly nothing there," he said. "Crystal used to wear a little gold cross, but I guess she had it on when she died." He opened his hand and showed me a silver and turquoise pin. "Maybe you'd like this."

I would have been more than happy to let Trace keep it, along with whatever pieces he wasn't telling me about. But I guessed he'd feel better if he gave me something. Besides, it would prove to Faye I'd searched the way she wanted me to.

"It's pretty," I said. "Thank you."

"You sure we inherit?" he asked. "I never inherited nothing before, except a shitload of trouble."

"That's what Sam told me," I said. "It's the law."

Trace shook his head. "The law never did me no favors before," he said. "If it's okay with you, I think I'll stick around, look things over. See if Budge or Crystal left some money or something. Course, I'll give you your share."

"Great," I said. "You look and I'll go back to Faye's."

"You sure?" he asked. "I can walk you home."

"No, that's okay," I said. "I have directions. But I'll see you tomorrow? At the funeral?"

"I'll be there," Trace said. "They were my sisters too."

nineteen

Pauline must have decided nothing I owned was appropriate for the funeral. Alyssa is six inches taller and twenty pounds heavier than me, so the outfit Pauline chose for me came from Brooke's closet. Black wool skirt, pale pink silk blouse, burgundy cashmere sweater. The skirt and sweater still had their price tags, so I had to borrow scissors from Faye to snip away proof of Val's generosity to her daughter.

"Why don't you wear Crystal's pin?" Faye asked. "Add a little color to the sweater?"

"I don't think so," I said, knowing it would feel like a double desecration. But the skirt had a pocket, and I slipped the pin in there. I guess that was an acceptable compromise to Faye, because she didn't press me about it.

Jack and the girls are Episcopalians, and when Mom and I go to church, we join them at St. James. Not that any of us go that often. But that's my image of a church, stately and formal. The kind of church Brooke's outfit belonged in.

New Hope Gospel Church looked nothing like that, but unlike practically everyplace else I'd seen in Pryor, it looked alive. It was a mile or so out of town, located in a desolate field that now served as a parking lot. Even though Faye and I had left early, the lot was almost completely full when we arrived, with cars and pickup trucks, and TV news vans. Faye found a spot, and as we walked toward the church, we both noticed oversize loudspeakers set up so the crowd outside could hear the service.

There were two police officers standing by the door. Faye walked up to one of them. "Hi, Joey," she said. "Are there any seats left?"

"It's all full," he replied. "Sorry, Faye. But they'll be broadcasting the whole thing. You can even sit in your car, like a drive-in, and hear what's going on."

I could see Faye was tempted to tell Joey who I was, but

the field was swarming with reporters and I gave her a shake of the head. She scowled but kept quiet.

"I'm sorry," she said to me. "I should've gotten us here earlier."

"It's okay," I said, because there was nothing else to say.

The crowd kept milling around, and news crews interviewed whoever they thought might provide a good story. The people of Pryor seemed happy to cooperate. Talking to reporters was the last thing I wanted to do, but I guess none of them thought I looked interesting enough. I was glad for that, and relieved, because other people were staring at me. Maybe they knew who was staying with Faye, or maybe it was because I was all Coffey, but I could sense their appraising looks.

Everything seemed to stop as Trace walked up to the church, accompanied by a tiny, sour-smelling old woman I recognized immediately as Granny Coffey. "Let us in," she said. "That's my flesh and blood in there."

"Yes, Mrs. Coffey," Joey said. "Hi, Trace. It's been a while."

Trace nodded. "Granny, that's Willa standing over there," he said, pointing to me.

Granny Coffey walked over to me. "Well, ain't you the high-class lady," she said. "What're you waiting for? Come on in."

I felt as though she'd yanked me by the ear, but it was Trace who took my hand and pulled me along.

The church was simple, more a barn than a cathedral, and it was jammed. I kept my head down, trying not to look at the front of the church, where a full-size coffin sat flanked by two little coffins to its right, another to its left, each with a photograph and covered with flowers. I could hear bits of conversation as we made our way to the front.

". . . such darling little girls . . ."

". . . saddest thing I ever saw . . ."

". . . her head right off. Heard they had to sew it back on."

". . . don't believe their nerve coming to this . . ."

Granny Coffey must have heard that one, because she turned around. "Those are my great-grandbabies up there," she said. "They bear my name. And these two are more their kin than any of you." She gestured wildly. "Now keep your traps shut and let us through."

The nervous chattering turned into silence. Granny Coffey, Trace, and I made our way to the front.

"Clear out room for us," she demanded when we got to the front row. "That's our kin up there."

"How dare you come?" a woman whispered. "When it was Dwayne who did this?"

"Think I don't know that?" Granny yelled. "Think my

heart ain't breaking from shame? Now show a little of that Christian charity you're always hollering about and leave us sit in our rightful place."

The woman looked distraught, but the man sitting next to her gestured to some of the people in the row and they cleared out. Granny, Trace, and I made our way in. Trace kept holding on to my hand; I'm not sure which one of us was comforting the other.

It was surrounded by noise, the voices of scores of strangers talking about people I should have known, should have loved. Most of the words I couldn't make out, but I did hear someone say something about jewelry, and I focused on that.

"They wanted Crystal's favorite pin for her dress," a woman said. "Turquoise and silver. But it was gone, along with most of her other jewelry. Someone must've broken in and taken it all."

"No one has any shame anymore," the woman sitting next to her said. "No respect for the living or the dead."

Instinctively my hand went into the skirt pocket. I felt for the tip of the pin, let it pierce my skin. I pulled my hand out before I left a bloodstain in Brooke's skirt.

A choir came out and began singing hymns. People joined in. I would have liked to have sung along, but I didn't know any of the songs. I guessed it didn't matter. The hymns were heartfelt and soothing, and staring at the choir helped stop me from looking at the coffins, especially those three tiny ones.

Granny Coffey kept muttering, but Trace paid her no mind. I opened my bag and located the tissue packet Faye had given me. I had no idea where Faye was, and realizing that made me feel even more alone.

I was at this funeral as a Coffey, and while that had been my intention when I first told Mom I was going, it felt frightening now. Not because everyone there hated the Coffey blood, but because I hated it too, even as it coursed through me.

All around me people were crying, but at least the conversations had stopped. The choir finished singing as a tall beefy man I recognized from TV as Pastor Hendrick walked to the pulpit. There was a microphone attached to it, but I had the feeling it wasn't necessary. Even Granny Coffey had ceased her mumbling.

"I see many familiar faces here," the pastor began. "Faces of people who knew and loved Crystal Ballard Coffey and her beloved daughters, Kelli Marie, Kadi, and Krissi. People who rejoiced at their christenings, their birthdays.

"But I also see new faces here, people I don't know. Maybe they knew Crystal or the girls outside the world of this church. Maybe they didn't know them at all but needed to be here, to bear witness. None of us were there when Christ was on the cross, but all here bear witness to it.

"I'm not here to talk about Crystal, about Kelli Marie and Kadi and Krissi. Others will do that, far more eloquently than I. They'll speak of the beauty of those girls' souls, of the joy they brought to their family, their friends. They'll talk from the bottomless well of their grief, and we'll weep with them and embrace them with the power of our love.

"No, I'm not going to talk about them, when others will do it so much better than I ever could. Instead, I'm going to talk about Dwayne Coffey."

There was a gasp, as though everyone exhaled in horror at the exact same moment. Trace clutched my hand even tighter.

"Since we heard the horrible news, people have been full of questions," Pastor Hendrick said. "They've come to me and said, 'I was there when Dwayne Coffey was saved. I was there when he accepted Christ as his savior. I was there, week after week, as he sat in this very church, prayed the same prayers I prayed, rejoiced in the word of the Lord just as I did. How could Dwayne have done this? How could a man, certainly one with failings, but a good Christian nonetheless, have done such a cruel, horrific act?'"

"Yes!" someone yelled from the back of the church. "How?"

"Less than a month ago, Dwayne Coffey was in this church, sitting where one of you now is," the pastor continued. "His wife and lovely little girls seated by his side. And when the service ended, and I stood outside, I saw Dwayne and asked him how he was. I knew about his battles with his demons. Many times we'd talked about them, prayed together.

"Crystal had turned her back to him, looking after the little girls, or pausing to talk to one of the many people who loved her. And Dwayne said to me, hardly louder than a whisper, 'Pastor Hendrick, my soul has died. I know it just as sure as I know the sky is blue.' He looked me straight in the eye when he said it, and I knew it was true. Souls can die before people. We've all seen that happen. We all know that sense of powerlessness we feel when someone we love is lost to Satan.

"We forget sometimes that accepting Christ as our savior isn't something we do once or twice in our lives. It's something we have to do every single moment of every single day. Just because Christ is in our heart doesn't mean Satan is satisfied to leave us alone. For Satan, no soul is off-limits. Not Dwayne's, not yours, not mine. Satan puts his temptations in all our paths. 'Look this way,' he says. 'Here's lust. Here's drink. Here's envy and anger, greed and resentment.' And all of us, not just Dwayne, but you and me, we all give in to those temptations at some point or another. We are all guilty.

We all allow Satan to chip away at our souls. Some days, with Christ's help, we're stronger than Satan. Some days, even with Christ at our side, Satan wins the battle.

"Yes, Dwayne Coffey was a Christian. I baptized him. I struggled with him against his demons. But Satan was stronger than Dwayne. And Dwayne's soul died.

"Satan may have won that battle," Pastor Hendrick continued. "But it was Crystal Ballard and her beautiful little daughters who won the war. Because we know when Dwayne raised his knife to them, their hearts and their souls went straight to heaven, straight to the loving embrace of their Father, their savior. The girls were too young to have sinned, too young for Satan to care about. And whatever sins Crystal might have committed in the everyday course of her everyday life, those sins were washed away in the blood she shed trying to save the lives of her precious daughters. Crystal Ballard died for the love of her children just as surely as Christ died for the love of us all.

"So as we grieve at our loss, our horrific loss, let us also rejoice for the four souls Satan cannot have. Let us celebrate God's power and give ourselves to it and vow to do battle against Satan in his many wicked forms. Let us vow to love with the purity of Crystal's love, the purity of those dear little girls' love, the purity of Christ's love. Now let us pray."

He began the recitation of the twenty-third Psalm, which

I recited along with Trace, with Granny Coffey, with everyone else in the church and most likely everyone else outside. I was comforted by the familiarity of the words, by the sense of being part of a whole far greater than me. And I was grateful that someone had offered an explanation I could understand for an act I could never truly understand.

Then a man walked to the pulpit. "I'm Michael Ballard," he said. "Crystal's brother." He took a deep breath. "I want to thank Pastor Hendrick for his words of wisdom. I was one of those full of questions. But through Christ's mercy, I have found an answer. Heaven must have been short four angels. God looked at all of us and found the four most perfect . . ." He began to weep and walked away.

A younger woman approached the pulpit. She was carrying a guitar.

"My name is Sarah Towner," she said. "Some of you know me from this church. Some of you know me from school. I was Kelli Marie's kindergarten teacher." She took a deep breath, and I could see she was fighting her tears. "Kelli Marie was a dear little girl, and she loved her mother and her baby sisters very much. She loved to sing. She told me once this was her favorite song. It's a song we sing in school, but Kelli Marie knew all the words before I taught it in class. She said she sang it all the time to Kadi and Krissi. So I'm singing it for all of them."

She began to strum her guitar and sing.

The itsy-bitsy spider
Climbed up the water spout
Down came the rain
And washed the spider out
Out came the sun
And dried up all the rain
And the itsy-bitsy spider
Climbed up the spout again

I started to cry, and my tears soon became sobs of hysteria. They couldn't be stopped. I had no control anymore. Everything halted, everyone stared, and I kept weeping, until finally Trace lifted me up and dragged me down the aisle, out of the church, into Faye's warm and accepting embrace.

twenty

"I'M GOING TO GET DRUNK," Faye informed me that night. "Not roaring, fall-on-the-floor drunk. Just drunk enough to forget the sight of those little coffins. I'm sorry, sweetie. It's not a Dairy Queen night. It's a getting-drunk night."

I nodded. Faye was already on her fourth beer, so she wasn't telling me something I hadn't guessed.

"Shame you can't get drunk," Faye said. "I'd offer you a beer or three, but Terri'd kill me."

"No, that's okay," I said. I'd made enough of a fool of myself that day without needing to get drunk on top of it.

Faye had started out drinking from a glass, but around

the third beer she went straight to the bottle. She took another swig. "Worst thing I ever saw," she said. "Not that I could see much from outside. More like what I felt I saw. We all felt it out there. We all felt those coffins, those poor little girls' coffins."

I thought about how the girls had shared a bedroom, the twins had shared a bed, and now they would share the earth beneath their tombstone, three little coffins, almost touching each other and their mother's, but separated for all eternity.

"You all right?" Faye asked me, not for the first time that evening.

"I'm fine," I said. "I'm sorry I lost control."

"I never saw anyone cry like you did today," Faye said. "It was like you were crying for the whole world."

I cringed. I had no business crying the way I had, no right. They were my sisters by blood only. They weren't like Brooke and Alyssa, whom I'd shared everything with for most of my life. No one who saw me could possibly think I was crying for Kelli Marie and Kadi and Krissi. They'd think I was a fraud. Why shouldn't they? That's what I thought.

"Good for you to cry," Faye said. "You keep things bottled up. Terri says that all the time, that you keep too much to yourself."

I bent down to scratch Moe's ears. I liked Moe. He didn't care who scratched his ears, just as long as someone did.

"You look like Budge," Faye said, starting on her fifth beer. "Your eyes, your mouth, they're Budge Coffey all over again. And maybe a little of you is like Budge. There was some goodness to him. I knew him most of his life. I saw the good along with the bad."

I had also. That made it almost worse, remembering the man who pushed me on the swing, who kissed me good night, who sang "Itsy-Bitsy Spider" every time I asked.

"But you're Terri's daughter," Faye said, "in every way that counts. Doesn't matter who you look like. Inside, you're like Terri."

I shrugged. There had been moments during the last few days when I felt like I understood Mom, Terri Doreen Penders Coffey McDougal. But there'd been more moments when I felt like I could never understand her. There were too many lies, too many unspoken truths.

Maybe I didn't want her to understand me either. Maybe I was afraid, always afraid, not just for the past few days but for every day since we escaped Pryor, that if Mom understood me, she'd see the Coffey in me and her love for me would curdle and die.

Faye put down her beer and stared at me. "Just like your momma," she said. "Terri'd rather cut her heart into a thousand little pieces than do something, say something, that might upset people. Jack. I mean Jack. And those spoiled-rotten daughters of his. She doesn't even want to upset their momma, who treats her no better than a nanny. 'Take the girls here. Take the girls there. Bandage their knees. Listen to their prayers.' Never let them know how she feels, though. Keeps all of that inside her."

"Mom doesn't feel like their nanny," I said. "She loves the girls. They love her. We're a family."

Faye snorted. "Family, my ass," she said. "Families fight. Wives fight. They don't just say 'Yes, Jack. Whatever you think, Jack.'"

"Jack doesn't like fights," I said. "He hates them."

"What does he have to fight about?" Faye asked. "He's got everything he wants. His daughters grab whatever they can get, and you and Terri are grateful for the crumbs. She worships the ground he walks on, and you act like he's a saint."

"He's not a saint," I said. "But we *are* lucky." I thought about Trace, drifting from home to home. I thought about Budge, unable to stop hurting me, about Grandma Coffey leaving me outside while she slept in a drunken stupor. I thought about Grandpa Penders, who cut Mom off forever because she took twenty dollars from his wallet so she could escape a dangerous husband.

I thought about Pryor, a town that killed its young.

"We *are* lucky," I said again. "Luckier than I ever knew."

Faye reached across the table to touch my hand. "Honey,

I know. I know Jack's a good man. Lord knows, Terri's told me often enough, all he's done for her, for you. But she turns her back to his bad side. She didn't used to. Before the girls moved in with you, before she gave up her life to care for those brats, she'd talk about Jack the way a wife talks about her husband. The good and the bad. And there was plenty of bad."

"Bad how?" I asked, a question I never would have asked a week before, or if Faye had been sober.

"Bad the way husbands can be," Faye said, finishing the beer and walking over to the refrigerator for what I hoped would be her last bottle of the night.

"Not bad like Budge," I said. "Jack's never hit Mom or me."

"No, hon, not like Budge," Faye said. "There's lots of ways a man can be bad. A man can be faithful and beat his wife senseless, or he can never raise a hand to his wife and cheat on her regular."

"Jack was unfaithful?" I asked. "Not to Mom."

"Not to her or with her," Faye said. "To that high and mighty first wife of his, years before he met Terri."

"I don't believe you," I said. "Jack's not the kind of man who'd do that."

Faye laughed. "They're all the kind who would," she said. "Some dream about it and some do the deed. Jack's case, he did the deed on a regular basis. When Brooke was a baby, he had an affair with a girl he worked with. Val got pregnant with Alyssa to try to hold on to him, but she caught him cheating again and that was the end of it. Val gave up on men, and Jack became Superdaddy. Then your momma walked in, and the rest is history." She laughed. "History," she said. "His story and her story."

"How do you know?" I asked. "You didn't know Jack then."

"Course not," Faye said. "Terri told me. First couple of years, she was worried sick he'd get tired of her, find someone else. He'd done it to Val, and Val had a lot more going for her as far as Terri could see."

"I don't want to hear this," I said. "I'm going to bed."

"Fine," Faye said. "Be like your momma. Turn your back on the truth. But the truth'll set you free. Budge. Jack. My exes. All of them. Men. Sinners all. No saints in this world, sweetie. Just different kinds of sinners."

twenty-one

ICALLED MOM on Thursday morning after Faye left for work. "Oh," she said, as though surprised to hear my voice. "I can't talk now, honey. We're picking the girls up in a few minutes. Our flight leaves at noon."

"Is everything okay?" I asked. "Has Brooke calmed down?"

"We're all fine," she said. "How was the funeral?"

"Horrible," I said.

"Well," Mom said. "You insisted."

"I know that, Mom," I said.

"I should get going," she said. "Jack's downstairs. I told him I'd meet him there in a minute."

"I'll see you tomorrow night," I said. "Have a safe flight."

"You too," Mom said. "Give Faye my love. And thank her for me, please."

"I love you," I said.

"I love you too, honey," Mom said. "And I've missed you. We'll have a long talk when you get back. Just the two of us. All right?"

"All right," I said. "See you tomorrow."

Mom hung up first. I stared at the phone, at the dozens of messages I'd ignored over the past week. This was as good a time as any to make my way through them. Most were from kids I knew from choir. Some were from kids I hardly knew at all. Three were from Lauren.

The first two were short messages, asking me how I was. The third message was a lot longer.

"Willa, I'm so worried about you," she said, the sound of her voice reminding me of how close we'd once been. "I called Brooke, but she said she hadn't spoken to you in days. I know I haven't been much of a friend lately. Everything feels so different here. I feel so different. And I won't blame you if you don't want to speak to me. But something like this, what Brooke told me . . . I feel sick I'm not there for you. I wish I could do something. I wish I'd been a better friend. Oh God, I'm going to start crying. I'm sorry, Willa. I love you, and I'm so sorry about everything."

I'd deleted all the other messages, but I kept Lauren's. I felt as though I'd spent the past week doing nothing but apologizing, to Mom, to Jack, to Pauline, to Faye, to the universe. I was sorry I was angry. I was sorry I was a Coffey. I was sorry I was the lucky one, the one who survived, the one who was never satisfied despite being the lucky one.

But Lauren was sorry too. Lauren, who in some ways reminded me of Brooke, getting what she wanted easily, gracefully. Brooke loved me because she had to. If we hadn't been stepsisters, sharing a home and parents, she wouldn't know I existed. But Lauren chose to be my friend.

I called her back, getting her voice mail. I was almost relieved, since I didn't know what I'd have said if she'd answered.

"It's Willa," I said. "I'm okay. I'm in Texas, but I'll be going home tomorrow." I tried to think how I could sum up everything I'd been through in the past few days in a way Lauren could understand. "I've learned so much about my family, about me. I don't think I'm different, though, just . . . I don't know. Sadder. Maybe smarter. It's been awful, but I'm glad I came, if that makes any sense. I'm really glad you called. It helped a lot to hear your voice. Take care. I'll see you when you get home."

I began washing the breakfast dishes, relieved to have a

job to do, however small. I'd just finished the last plate when I heard the doorbell ring. I dried my hands on Faye's dishtowel and walked to the front door.

Trace stood there. "I wanted to see how you're doing," he said.

"I'm okay," I replied. "Embarrassed but okay."

"You got nothing to be embarrassed about," he said. "You wasn't the only person who lost it yesterday."

"I wouldn't know," I said. "I was too hysterical to see anyone else. Want to come in? Faye made coffee if you'd like some."

"No, that's okay," he said. "I was wondering if you wanted to go to the cemetery. You didn't get there yesterday, and I thought maybe you'd want to before you go."

"It's a long walk," I said.

"I borrowed Granny's car," Trace said. "She's sleeping it off, so if we hurry, she won't even know it's gone."

My guess was everyone in Pryor was sleeping it off or wishing they could.

"Yes," I said. "I'd like that. Thank you."

I grabbed my jacket and bag and joined Trace. We walked over to Granny Coffey's car. It was filthy, inside and out, reeking of stale cigarette smoke, spilled beer, and pee. I wondered if Trace could strap me on the roof so I wouldn't have to sit inside.

But he seemed oblivious to the mess and the stink. "The seat belts don't work," he said. "But I promise to drive real careful."

I remembered my last trip to the cemetery and hoped Trace understood the rationale behind stop signs.

He drove cautiously and the drive seemed to take forever. I rolled the window down and that helped a little.

"So when do you leave?" he asked.

"Tomorrow," I said. "Pauline's arriving tonight and we'll go in the morning."

"Who's Pauline?" he asked, taking what felt like half an hour before driving through a four-way stop.

"A friend of my family," I said. "She came down with me so I wouldn't be alone."

"That's real nice of her," Trace said.

"Yes," I said. "It was real nice of her."

"Faye's a friend too," he said. "To your momma and to Budge."

I nodded.

"Budge always liked her," Trace said. "He used to say it was a damn shame the men she got involved with."

My mother used to say the same thing. But I felt disloyal saying that, so I just nodded.

"Are you going to be staying long?" I asked. "Or will you be going home to Memphis?"

"Memphis ain't home," Trace said. "I don't got a home, not like you mean. Never have. All I got are places."

"Do you think you'll stay here, then?" I asked. "Move back in with Granny?"

"Gets awful cold sleeping on the porch," he said. "I'm staying at Budge's till the rent runs out. Look around, see if there's anything there I could turn into cash. You mind about that? It's half yours."

I still felt guilt-stricken over the turquoise pin. "I don't mind," I said.

"I took the guitar already," Trace said. "It's in the back."

"Good," I said. "I don't know how to play."

"He would've taught you, same as me," Trace said. "If you'd stuck around. Budge wasn't good for much, except playing the guitar and making babies."

And killing, I thought. Budge had a real gift for killing.

"And hurting," Trace said. "He was real good at that."

"What do you do in Memphis?" I asked. "What kind of work do you do?"

"This and that," he said. "People want things, I help out."

"What kind of things?" I asked.

"Things a nice girl like you don't want to know about," he replied.

"Legal things?" I persisted.

"What is this?" Trace asked. "You a cop now? I do what

I need to. I made it through yesterday and I'm alive today. Which is more than you can say for these three little girls we're going visiting."

"I'm sorry," I said. "I know so little about you."

"Did you ever think maybe it's better that way?" he said.

"No," I said. "I never thought that."

Trace made the turn to the cemetery. "You got nothing to be sorry about," he said. "I'm the one who's sorry. I used to think about you a lot when you were little. You turned out better than I expected. Like Granny Coffey said, you're a lady. Your folks did a real good job raising you."

"You used to think about me?" I said. "Does that mean you stopped?"

"I reckon I did stop," Trace replied. "I asked about you once, wondered how you were, if Budge ever heard from you. Big mistake. It set him off bad. After that, I was scared to even think about you, let alone ask."

"Couldn't people tell?" I asked. "That he hurt you, I mean."

"I got real good at lying," Trace said. "And most times I deserved what I got."

"I don't believe that," I said. "No one deserves what Budge did."

"Well, he's not around to do it no more," Trace said. "Now, I bet you're a good girl. Never get into trouble."

"I guess so," I said. "I mean, I guess I'm good."

"You stay like that," Trace said. "Stay pure. Don't let boys have their way with you. Because they'll lie to get what they want. How about drugs?"

"What do you mean?" I asked.

"You ever mess with drugs?" he said.

I shook my head.

"Good," he said. "'Cause drugs work for a moment, make you feel like everything's all right after all, and then they wear off and you're stuck in the same shit hole you always were. You listen to Momma Terri. She knows what's best for you. No drugs. No boys."

I wanted to laugh, but I was afraid Trace would never forgive me if I did. "I'll do my best," I said. "I wish I'd had you around to give me advice."

"No you don't," he said. "You don't want no one like me around. Everything I learned, I learned the hard way. You're better off with that pretty family of yours. Just listen to what I'm telling you and don't make my mistakes."

"I promise," I said.

Trace drove the car through the cemetery gates. I thought it might be the last time I'd see him, the last chance I'd have to ask him one final thing.

"Trace?" I said, trying to make it sound casual, like I

didn't care what the answer was. "After that time you asked about me, and Budge got so mad, did he ever mention Mom or me again?"

"Just once that I can remember," he said. "I was living with him and Crystal. He got a letter from your momma. He went half crazy, shouting about what a no-good . . . Well, he said some bad things about your momma. And I got mad and told him Momma Terri wasn't anything like what he said, and that really set him off. He started walloping anything that stood in his way. Then he went off on a three-day drunk, and Crystal said it was all my fault for picking a fight with him and I had to get out and stay out. I hung around Granny Coffey's for a few days after that, thinking once Budge sobered up, he'd ask me back, but he never did. I blame Crystal for that. Budge used to like having me around, no matter how mad he got, but Crystal turned him against me. I never saw him again, or the babies." He stopped the car under a cottonwood tree. "Good. There's no one here. You ready?"

I realized with a start that I wasn't. It had been hard enough seeing those four little headstones that represented Mom's stillborn brothers and sisters. They were decades old, moss covered, as much a part of the cemetery as Grandpa and Grandma Penders's graves had been.

"Give me a minute," I said.

"Take your time," he said. "They ain't going nowhere."

"You must hate him," I said. "What he did to them, to you."

"Yeah," Trace said. "But I love him too. Or I did. I sure wanted him to love me. Hell, I wanted *someone* to love me, and he was the best shot I had." He laughed. "Don't say much about the circles I travel in, now does it."

"You're my brother," I said. "I love you."

"I'm lucky, then," he said. "I got the best Budge had to give. His guitar and you. Think you can handle this?"

"If you help me," I said.

We got out of the car, Trace opening the back door and pulling out the guitar. Then we walked a few feet toward the four freshly dug graves. They were covered with flowers, so there was almost no dirt to be seen, but they still seemed raw and unprotected.

"I don't know who'll pay for the tombstones," Trace said. "Most likely Crystal's folks. They'll want something pretty for them. That'll be nice for the girls. Angels maybe."

"Maybe we should have brought flowers," I said.

"They have enough," Trace said. "Heaven's full of flowers. I thought they might like a song instead. I used to sing to Kelli Marie all the time when she was a baby. Calmed her right down."

"What?" I asked. "What song?"

"Don't worry," Trace said. "Not 'Itsy-Bitsy Spider.' I don't want to have to carry you out of here."

I managed to laugh.

"Maybe a hymn," he said. "You have a favorite? Budge taught me some after he found Jesus."

"I love 'Amazing Grace,'" I said. "That's a hymn, isn't it?"

"Yeah," Trace said. "Budge's favorite. But Crystal hated it. Maybe we should sing something else."

"I don't really know any other hymns," I said.

"Well, it don't have to be no hymn," Trace said. "Just something pretty the girls would like." He strummed a chord. "'Silent Night,' maybe? It's not a hymn, but it sounds like one. You think it's okay to sing it in April?"

"I love 'Silent Night,'" I said. "It's my favorite carol any time of year."

"Mine too," he said. "It makes me glad for baby Jesus, that he had a momma who loved him." He began the song in a surprisingly pure tenor.

Silent night. Holy night.

All is calm. All is bright.

Years of singing in choirs had taught me how to harmonize. I let Trace sing the next two lines, the ones he loved.

Round yon Virgin Mother and Child

Holy infant, so tender and mild

And then I joined in, our two voices singing to the north Texas wind. Singing to the angels. Singing to the dead.

Sleep in heavenly peace.

Sleep in heavenly peace.

part three
[love and money]

twenty-two

IT WAS AFTER MIDNIGHT by the time Pauline pulled up to my house. But the porch light was on, and between that and the street light, I could sense the violence that had happened just a few days earlier. The grass had been trampled on, and the green of spring growth had a brownish stain to it, the stain of blood from knives and bullets.

Pauline walked silently by my side. Jack must have been watching for us, because he opened the door before I had a chance to pull out my key. He hugged Pauline and thanked her, then embraced me as though it had been a lifetime since he'd seen me last.

"You going to be okay?" Pauline asked me.

"I'm fine," I said. "I don't know how to thank you."

"I did it for me too," she said. "I'll call you tomorrow." She looked at her watch. "I mean today. Try to get some sleep."

"You too," I said, kissing her goodbye. I couldn't imagine how I would have gotten home without her. She never pushed with questions, just listened to the little I could say and seemed to understand all my silences.

"Terri's asleep," Jack said, as we watched Pauline drive away. "She was all right in Orlando, but it's been tough on her since we got back. She's taking sedatives and they've made it hard for her to stay awake. The girls are sleeping also. I'm sorry, pumpkin. This isn't much of a homecoming for you."

"I wasn't expecting a party," I said. "I'm sorry. That didn't come out right."

"It's okay," Jack said. "Would you like a cup of tea? Something to eat?"

I shook my head. "I think I'll go straight to bed," I said. "I'll feel more like talking in the morning."

Jack hugged me again. "We have a lot to talk about," he said. "Including adoption. It's about time you became a McDougal."

"In the morning," I said. "I love you, Jack."

"Love you right back," he said.

I tiptoed into my bedroom, but it didn't matter. Alyssa was sitting in bed, her laptop resting against her knees.

"You know he cut Krissi's head off," she said, looking over to me. "He had her head in his left hand and the knife in his right hand, and he dropped the head and slashed the cop. Then they shot him."

"Mom says it didn't happen that way," I said.

"She's lying," Alyssa said. "Everyone says that's what happened."

Part of me wanted to say Mom didn't lie, but the past week had taught me she didn't always tell the truth. Still, I didn't like hearing Alyssa call her a liar.

"How was Orlando?" I asked.

"Horrible," Alyssa said. "Mom and Daddy fought the entire time. What was it like in Texas? Do you know why your father did it? Not the head. Everything. Do you know why he killed your sisters?"

"I'm really tired," I said. "I've been traveling all day, Alyssa."

"I know all about traveling," she replied. "I just thought you might want to talk about it. He is your father, after all."

I hated her. I hated her tennis and her sweaters and her trips around the world. I'd never let myself think that before, because she was my sister in everything but name, and you love your sisters. Even when they're selfish and spoiled, you love them. If you want them to love you, you have to love them.

I wanted to tell Alyssa how much I hated her, how long I'd hated her, but if I did, she'd tell Jack, and for all his talk about how I was his daughter, I wasn't. Alyssa was, and his loyalties were with her and Brooke, first and always. And Mom's loyalties were with Jack.

"I don't know why," I said, opening my suitcase so I wouldn't have to look at her. "What did Jack and your mom fight about?" That was a question I never would have asked her before. But I couldn't help remembering what Faye and her beer had told me.

"They fought about everything," Alyssa said. "Terri. You. Mom doesn't think Daddy should adopt you. They fought about me, but they always fight about me. They fought about Brooke too, and they never fight about her."

"That sounds like fun," I said, regretting not having done a load of laundry at Faye's as she'd suggested. What clean clothes I had I put into my chest of drawers.

Alyssa laughed. "I'm going to miss you, Willa," she said. "I won't miss Brooke, but I'll miss you."

"You're just going to Brussels for a week," I said. "I'll be here when you get back."

"Not Brussels," she said. "After Brooke's graduation. I'll miss you then."

I wasn't going to miss her, but I didn't say so. "I'll be here when you get back in September," I said. "It's only a couple of months."

"That's what I'm telling you," she said. "I won't be back. That's why I'll miss you."

"Where are you going to be?" I asked, draping Brooke's clothes over a chair and hanging mine up in my part of the closet.

"Daddy didn't tell you?" Alyssa said. "I'm moving to Florida."

"To live with your mother?" I asked.

"To go to the tennis academy," Alyssa said. "Mom wants me to live with her, but I decided not to. There's a boarding school practically next door to the academy. All the kids go there."

"I thought Jack said you couldn't do that," I said. "Not for another year."

"I know," Alyssa said. "But Mom made the appointment at the academy, and since Daddy was there, we went on Tuesday. Mom and Daddy and me. Brooke stayed home."

I turned my light off and began undressing. That was how I did it, so Alyssa couldn't see my cut wounds, but this time it was so I didn't have to look at her.

"It was wonderful there," Alyssa said, talking into the darkness. "They told Daddy and Mom I was being held back living here, and if I had better coaches and practice partners and more court time, I'd be top ten already. And if I worked hard, I could be seeded at Junior Wimbledon next June. They'll recommend agents for Daddy and Mom to interview, and the agent'll find sponsors for me, and endorsement deals. I bet I'll be making more money than Mom in a couple of years."

"And Jack agreed to all that?" I asked, crawling into bed, already missing the comforting sensation of Curly nestling by my side. "Tennis academy? Boarding school? Agents?"

"Not at first," Alyssa said. "Daddy said I was too young, because that's what he always says, only this time Mom said I shouldn't be living with him and Terri anyway, that it wasn't safe for Brooke and me, because of your father, and what can you expect when you marry someone, well, when you marry someone like Terri. You know. Because she was married to someone like your father, even if it was a long time ago, and Daddy was never supposed to have full custody, and she was sick and tired of making mortgage payments for him and Terri. So I said I wanted to move to Florida more than anything, but I didn't want to live with Mom, and it made much more sense for me to go to boarding school, which was what they'd said at the academy. So Mom and Daddy stopped yelling at each other and they began yelling at me instead, and Brooke came out and told them to stop screaming and she didn't blame me for not wanting to live with either of them. She said if they stopped fighting with each other and thought about us for a change, they'd realize how much they were hurting us."

"Brooke said that?" I asked.

"She didn't shout or anything," Alyssa replied. "I can yell and scream and no one pays any attention, but when Brooke talks, it's like the whole world stops and listens. So we all calmed down long enough for me to say that I'd love to keep living with Daddy if I could only get the coaching I needed and I'd love to live with Mom, except I know how much she has to travel, and I don't know if either one of them believed me, but finally they said yes. And then Mom told Brooke she could go to USC, and Daddy looked like he was going to fight some more, but he didn't, so we both won."

"Congratulations," I said.

"I will miss you," she said. "Terri too. I wouldn't move away if it was just to live with Mom. I wish sometimes I was like Brooke. Everything comes so easy for her. But the only thing I'm really good at is tennis, and I'll do anything I have to to get better at it."

I didn't hate her anymore. Maybe I never had. Not even Budge had hated his family all the time.

"I'll miss you too," I whispered, but she'd already closed her eyes and turned her head away from me, as though I had never really been part of her life.

twenty-three

I KNOCKED ON BROOKE'S DOOR the next morning, being particularly careful not to open it until she said "Come in."

"I borrowed some clothes from you," I said, handing her the sweater, blouse, and skirt. "Do you want me to hang them up?"

"No, just leave them," she said.

I draped them over a chair. "Alyssa says it's definite," I said. "She's moving to Florida and you're going to USC."

"That's the plan," Brooke said. "I haven't sent my letters of intent yet."

"It's so far away," I said.

"Not far enough," Brooke said. "But it's the best I could do."

"Why do you need to get away?" I asked. "You're not in any danger. It's all over."

"It's not over for either one of us, and you know it," Brooke said. "School will be a nightmare on Monday. Coach is furious because I missed the match on Friday, but I couldn't face going back. Everybody'll be careful around you, but they're going to be all over me, asking me what happened, what I know. Like I know anything. Like it was my father and not yours. I begged Mom to let me go to Munich with her, but Dad went ballistic. He said I've missed enough school already, but that was just an excuse. He doesn't want you going to school alone on Monday. You'd think he'd know by now we don't have any classes together."

"I'm sorry," I said. "I'm sorry about all of it. I'm sorry I took your clothes. If you want, I'll burn them."

"No, that's okay," she said. "I'll just put them in the rummage pile."

I stared at her.

"Oh, no," Brooke said. "I didn't mean it that way. I'm sorry, Willa. I really am. The past couple of weeks, they've been horrible."

"They haven't been a lot of fun for me either," I said.

"No," Brooke said. "Of course not. Willa, this isn't about

you. I mean, it is about you, but it's not all about you. I need distance from Dad, from Mom, from everybody."

I thought about how desperate Mom had been to escape Pryor. Even in high school, she knew what her future would be if she stayed. Dead-end job. Abusive husband. No money. No hope.

Brooke was going from one cocoon to another. Taking her cashmere sweaters with her.

"Look," she said. "I know Daddy loves you. And that's good. I'm glad he does, and that he loves Terri, and you all love each other. You're a family, even if Alyssa and I are kind of add-ons."

"Add-ons?" I said. "Everything revolves around you."

Brooke shook her head. "Everything revolves around Daddy," she said. "Keeping him happy. Letting him dictate. It doesn't matter that all my friends have cars, and Mom would pay for it. Dad and Terri couldn't afford a car for you, so I shouldn't have one either. Or Fairhaven. That was even worse. I loved it there. But Daddy said it wasn't right for me to go to private school if you couldn't. Alyssa got to go there because of her schedule. But there was no reason for me to stay at Fairhaven, and you'd given up your home and your school and your friends, just for Alyssa and me. He made it sound like I'd be a monster if I stayed at my own school."

"I didn't know," I said. "I never asked him to say that."

"I know you feel like I get everything I want," Brooke said. "I'm not insensitive, Willa. No matter what Dad thinks. But there's a lot I've wanted and never had. A mother I can count on. Time alone with my father. Not having to feel careful all the time, like if I said one wrong thing, out I'd go."

"Your parents love you," I said. "They worship you."

"Sure," Brooke said. "When I get A's. When I'm All-State on the violin or winning at dressage or lacrosse. But Mom's only interested if I come in first. And Daddy loves you and Terri a lot more than he loves me."

"That's not true," I said. "You're his daughter. You mean everything to him."

"As long as I behave myself," Brooke said. "Know my place."

I laughed.

"This isn't a joke, Willa," Brooke said. "Not for me. It never has been for me. Remember that big fight we got into years ago?"

"I don't remember ever fighting with you," I said. "You must have dreamed it."

"Oh, no," Brooke said. "I didn't dream it. I was six or seven. Alyssa and I kept some of our toys at Daddy's, for when we visited, and Mom said I could still keep stuff with him now that you and Terri were there, but I should make sure you didn't play with our toys or wear our clothes. They were ours, not yours."

"I knew that," I said. "I wasn't allowed in your room unless you invited me. Mom was really firm about that."

"Well, you must not have cared," Brooke said. "Because I came over one day and I found you playing with my dolls. So I grabbed a doll from you and you threw something at me and I started hitting you. We really went at each other. You sure you don't remember?"

I shook my head. "I remember your dolls," I said. "And a dollhouse. I loved it when you'd come over and we played with your dollhouse. But I don't remember any fight."

"Terri tried to break it up," Brooke said. "But she couldn't. Alyssa had thrown herself into it. Remember how she used to bite? Daddy came in, and it must have seemed like two against one. I don't think I've ever seen him that angry. Not until this week. Alyssa was screaming and you were crying, and Daddy picked me up and carried me to the car and drove me back to Mom's. He exiled me. I never forgave him."

It came back to me. I could hear Brooke shrieking as Jack dragged her from the house. I could picture Alyssa, not yet four, hysterical on the living room floor.

Mom pushed me into my bedroom, slapped me hard

against my cheek, and slammed the door as she left. Over the sounds of my sobs, I could hear her comforting Alyssa.

But Alyssa didn't calm down. She kept screaming for her mommy, for her daddy, for Brooke. Then Jack came back and took Alyssa outside, where they played as though nothing had happened.

Mom came into my room then. I was in a state of rage. I yelled that she loved Brooke and Alyssa more than she loved me, that all I wanted was to go back home and be with Daddy and Granny Coffey.

Mom began shaking me. "Is that what you want?" she screamed. "You want to be treated like this?" She slapped me again, harder than I ever remember being hit, even by Daddy at his worst.

Then she burst into tears, and I was the one who comforted her, insisted it was all my fault, begged her to love me and let me stay.

Jack and Alyssa came back in. Mom wiped away her tears and kissed me again and again. "Don't tell Jack," she said. "I promise I'll never hit you again if you don't tell Jack. Promise me right now you'll never tell him."

"I promise," I said. "Just don't send me back to Daddy."

I heard her go to the bathroom, splash water on her face, and run downstairs. I stayed alone in my bedroom until my face didn't sting anymore and I felt like I could breathe again.

When I went to the kitchen, I found Mom, Jack, and Alyssa behaving as though nothing had happened. Jack was stirring a pot of spaghetti sauce. He put the ladle down, picked me up, and gave me a big kiss on my still-red cheek. I winced.

"Brooke really hit you hard," he said. "But don't worry, Willa. She and I had a long talk, and she knows better than to ever hurt you again."

I could feel Mom's eyes boring into me. I didn't want Jack to think Brooke had been the one to slap me, but if I told him the truth, Mommy might send me back to Daddy.

I burst out crying.

"Oh, pumpkin," Jack said, kissing my cheek and stroking my hair. "Brooke was a bad girl, but sisters can be like that. You forgive her, don't you?"

I sniffled a yes.

"Say, 'I love you, Jack,'" he instructed me.

"I love you, Jack," I said.

He laughed. "Love you right back," he said, gently putting me down on the floor. "Now go help Terri and Lyssie set the table."

I could have told Brooke all of this. But I wasn't about to play My Suffering Is Greater Than Your Suffering. It's a game I'd already lost to Trace and Kelli Marie and Kadi and Krissi.

Besides, Mom never hit me again. We both had lived up to our promises.

"So that's why you're going to USC?" I said instead. "Because Jack sent you home to your mother's?"

"I don't want to be here when Daddy adopts you," Brooke said. "I don't. It hurts how much he loves you, how easy he loves you. I can deal with it when I think of you as someone I share a house with. But I'm not ready for you to be my sister. I'm sorry, Willa, but I'm not."

"I'm not Sweetbriar," I said. "You can't just discard me."

But looking at the sister I'd both idolized and betrayed, I was no longer so sure she couldn't.

twenty-four

"Hi," mom said. "Am I interrupting? "

Actually she was. It was Sunday morning and Jack had insisted on taking Brooke and Alyssa to church. Mom was in the kitchen, trying to catch up with her schoolwork, and I had taken advantage of an empty house to go to the den and use the computer.

First, I'd written an e-mail to Lauren, trying to describe what Pryor had been like. It was easier to focus on that than to try to describe how I'd felt learning about Budge, my sisters, Trace. That would come at some point, maybe when Lauren came back. Maybe by then, I'd understand everything I was feeling—the sorrow, the fear, even the hope.

But for now, I limited myself to a brief and unflattering description of my behavior at the funeral. Lauren had been my best friend since I moved to Westbridge. I wouldn't have wanted her to see me act like that, but with her an ocean away, I felt safe telling her about my hysteria.

Once I pressed Send, I turned my attention to trying to locate Uncle Martin. Somewhere I had an uncle, an aunt, and eight cousins. The time had come to introduce myself to them, with or without Mom's knowledge and consent.

"Come on in," I said. "I just finished sending an e-mail to Lauren."

"You have a lot to tell her," Mom said. "So much has happened in the past couple of weeks. We haven't really talked since the motel."

That was true enough. After my confrontation with Brooke, I hadn't been too chatty. I'd spent most of Saturday doing ten days' worth of schoolwork and telling myself repeatedly that cutting wouldn't solve anything.

"I'm still not sure I'm ready to talk about Pryor," Mom said. "And there are other things we need to discuss."

"I guess it's still too disturbing for you," I said. "Budge dying. The way they asked you to identify his body."

To my surprise, Mom shook her head. "I know that's

what Jack thinks," she said. "But I'm glad Budge is dead. I'm glad I saw his body, so I'll never have to doubt. I used to dream about killing him, but I knew I'd lose you if I did. So I ran away. But I was still scared of him, what he might do to us. No, what's been upsetting me is knowing how close he came. I don't know what might have happened if Faye hadn't called the police."

"I remembered things about him when I was in Pryor," I said. "Not all of them bad. But I remember him hurting you."

"I could have lived with that," she said. "I did live with it. But he hurt you too. It took me a while to understand how bad that was. It was how I'd been punished when I was a kid. It was how I punished you. But Budge couldn't control it. I was terrified one day I wouldn't be able to stop him. So I ran. Budge didn't hurt you anymore. I took over for him."

"You haven't hit me in years," I said. "I hardly remember that you ever did."

"I was so scared Jack would find out," Mom said. "I knew how he felt about violence, about punishments. I was sure he'd see what damaged goods I was, how little I deserved him. Then we'd be on our own again. Jack was our protection, from Budge, from Pryor, from everything, really."

"We're safe now," I said. "We're in our home and we're safe."

"We're safe," Mom said. "But I have to talk to you about

our home. Jack doesn't have the heart. It's better if I explain."

"I know about Alyssa and Brooke," I said. "It's going to be you and Jack and me next year. I don't mind."

"It's more complicated than that," Mom said. "It's about money, our financial situation."

"What about it?" I asked.

"Val earns a lot of money," Mom said. "A lot more than Jack. Val pays for most of the girls' expenses. Jack pays his share, but it's more the day-to-day things, food, utilities. Val pays Alyssa's tuition and her tennis coaches, and for the country club and the violin lessons and Sweetbriar."

"I know that, Mom," I said.

"Val also pays for the house," Mom said. "That was the arrangement she and Jack made when she got transferred to Shanghai. She covered the down payment and pays three quarters of the mortgage. Jack pays the rest."

I remembered what Alyssa said about Val being tired of paying the mortgage and started to feel sick.

"We knew things would be tighter when Brooke went to college," Mom said. "But Val agreed to keep paying her share of the mortgage for the first year after that. Alyssa would stay with us until you graduated high school. Then she'd move back with Val, we'd sell the house, and Jack and I would find someplace we could afford. I was hoping to have my degree by then, and with both our salaries, we'd do okay. Jack would pay child support for Alyssa and help out with Brooke's college expenses, but we figured if we were very careful, we'd find a way to help you with your tuition. Especially if Brooke got an athletic scholarship. What we'd save in her tuition, we hoped to apply to yours."

"I'm not worried about college," I said, frantically trying to keep Mom from telling me what I knew was coming. "I always figured I'd work my way through. And I can pay off college loans. It's okay, Mom. I never thought it would be handed to me."

"I'm glad, honey," Mom said. "But that's only part of it. With Alyssa leaving in July, Val's payments are going to stop altogether. And with Brooke going to USC, her expenses are going to be a lot higher than we prepared for. I'll leave school and get a job. But even with that, we won't be able to afford this house."

"I'll be getting Social Security," I said. "We could use that for the mortgage."

Mom shook her head. "I spoke to Sam Whalen, and he told me how much to expect. It won't be nearly enough. This house costs a fortune, Willa. The mortgage and taxes. There's no way we could afford it without Val's help."

I wasn't looking forward to school on Monday, to being stared at and who knew what else. But it was my school with my teachers and my friends, and most important, my choir. No one wants to start a new school their senior year.

"Can we buy someplace close by?" I asked. "Or even rent? Can't we rent someplace in Westbridge just for a year?"

"I don't think so, honey," Mom said. "We can't buy anywhere unless Jack gets a loan from his parents, which he refuses to do. What little there is to rent around here is way beyond what we can afford. I don't know where we'll be moving to, but it's not going to be anywhere near here."

I willed myself not to cry. I'd cried enough about things I knew were more important. "When will we move?" I asked. "Right after Brooke's graduation?"

"That's when we'll put the house on the market," Mom said. "Once the girls leave. It's less disruptive that way, and besides, it's a good idea to let a little time pass, give people a chance to forget what happened. But we can't afford Jack's share of the mortgage and rent on an apartment. We'll move the day someone closes on the house."

"That could be anytime," I said. "This summer. Next winter. I could start a new school halfway through the year." Like I had four years ago, I realized. No one had cared then either. "Mom, that's so unfair. You've got to see how unfair it is."

"You think I don't know that?" Mom said. "But you're not Val's daughter. She has no obligation to help you out. And frankly, you've benefited a lot from her over the past few years. So have I. We've had this house, and I got three years of college instead of working."

"I never asked for this house," I said. "And it's not like you graduated. Brooke and Alyssa get everything. They always have. Alyssa isn't even going to live with Val. And Brooke doesn't have to go to USC. She could accept the scholarship to North Carolina. They get everything, and I get nothing. That's how it's always been."

For a moment, I thought Mom was going to hit me. I think she thought so too. Her voice was shaky when she finally spoke. "Don't ever say that to Jack," she said. "And let me tell you something. I got this house for us, for you. There was another one in Smithton that Jack and Val both thought we should buy. It was bigger, and closer to Fairhaven. I was the one who insisted on this house. The other one had four bedrooms, but one was really small, and I convinced Jack that Val would insist Brooke and Alyssa get the bigger rooms and that wouldn't be fair to you. Then I convinced Val that the Smithton school system wasn't as good and if Brooke or Alyssa decided to leave Fairhaven, they'd be better off here. I was determined to send you to Westbridge because it's known for its drama department and its choir. That was the only thing I could give you, Willa, and I saw to it you got it. I wish we could stay here. I wish you could graduate with your class. But you've had a lot more than you're entitled to, and I don't want you to forget it."

"Do the girls know?" I asked, thinking about how resentful Brooke was. This was a hell of a way to pay me back for playing with her doll.

"Jack's telling them today after church," she said. "We decided to do it that way. The girls will be moving on, so they won't care. And Jack couldn't bear to tell you himself. He loves you so much, honey. It breaks his heart to see you unhappy."

twenty-five

I WAS DEBATING how to sign the e-mail I'd written to Uncle Martin when Brooke stuck her head in the room. "Are you busy?" she asked.

I typed in "Your niece, Willa Coffey," pressed Send, and shut down the computer. There was no reason to hide the e-mail from Brooke, but there was no reason to tell her about it either.

It had taken a while to track Uncle Martin down, but I finally located a Martin Penders in Blatchersville, Idaho. He owned a taxidermy business, complete with an e-mail address. There was a chance, I supposed, it wasn't the right Martin

Penders, but it was still worth the try. I'd decide what to tell Mom if I heard back from him.

"I found this when I was hanging up my skirt," Brooke said, handing me Crystal's pin. "It was in the pocket."

"Oh, yeah," I said. "I forgot about it."

"It's pretty," she said. "Did you buy it in Pryor?"

"More like I stole it," I said. "No, I'm joking. I had as much right to it as anybody." I remembered how Crystal's family had wanted it for her and wished I could make the pin disappear, along with Brooke.

Brooke sat down on the sofa. "Daddy told us about selling the house," she said. "I'm sorry, Willa."

"It's okay," I said, swiveling the chair so I faced her. "It's not your fault."

"No," she said. "I'm sorry about everything. I didn't mean any of those things I said about Daddy adopting you. I hope you believe me, Willa. You're my sister, every bit as much as Alyssa, and I'm happy that Dad's going to adopt you. I hope there's a big party."

"It's not going to happen anytime soon," I said. "I'm getting Social Security from Budge until I'm eighteen, and I can use the money."

"That's great," Brooke said. "Can you use it for the mortgage?"

"It's not enough," I said. "I already asked Mom."

"Oh," she said. "Well, Daddy can adopt you on your eighteenth birthday. You could have a really big party then."

"I guess," I said. "Right now I'm kind of fathered out."

"Me too," Brooke said. "Daddy and Mom were horrible in Orlando. He and Terri never fight. It's like he's a different person when he's with Mom. It's a nightmare."

I tried to picture Val as a young wife and mother, trying desperately to save her marriage, knowing her husband was unfaithful to her. But all I could imagine was Mom trying to escape Budge before he hurt us again.

"Budge was pretty violent," I said. "I think Mom decided when she married Jack that she'd do anything to avoid fighting with him."

"There's got to be a balance," Brooke said. "Do you think we'll find it?"

"No," I said. "Do you?"

"I hope so," Brooke said. She glanced at the door and lowered her voice. "Alyssa thinks you cut yourself," she said. "She mentioned it to me months ago, but she thought you'd been doing it even longer than that."

"She doesn't have to worry," I said. "It's not contagious."

"Does Daddy know?" Brooke asked. "Or Terri? Or Lauren?"

I shook my head.

"Maybe you should talk to someone about it," she said.

"It's no big deal," I said. "It's not like drugs. I'm not addicted. I only do it when I'm really stressed out."

Brooke looked even more uncomfortable.

"What?" I said. "Lots of kids cut, but they don't have fathers that slashed their families to death?"

"That wasn't what I was thinking," she said. "I just don't like the idea that I'm adding to your stress."

"Then let's change the subject," I said.

"Okay," Brooke said. "Let's. Because this isn't about you cutting or stress. Honestly, Willa. It's something I've been thinking about for a couple of days now. The way Dad and Mom were fighting, I knew something was going on, and then Dad told us today he's putting the house on the market this summer. He didn't say so, but I know it's because I'm turning down the scholarship."

"That's only part of it," I said.

"It's the part I can do something about," Brooke replied. "If you want, I'll go to North Carolina and play lacrosse for another year. If I hate it, I can transfer, but in the meantime you'll be able to graduate with your class."

"You would do that for me?" I asked.

"I love you," she said. "And it isn't fair for you to get cheated out of senior year here."

I tried to figure it out. If Jack had less to pay in tuition and I chipped in my Social Security, maybe we could afford the house.

But Mom would still have to quit school to work full-time. Brooke would be unhappy at North Carolina and Mom would be unhappy because she couldn't finish her degree and Jack would be unhappy because he'd feel like he failed all of us.

It was hard to imagine me happy under those circumstances.

"Have you told Jack?" I asked.

Brooke shook her head. "I wanted to discuss it with you first," she said. "Tomorrow's going to be really rough at school, and you might decide you don't want to stay."

Which, of course, was what Brooke wanted. Not for the kids at school to be horrible, but for me to decide I'd be happier someplace where no one knew about Budge and me.

I could see her point. But no matter what, I'd be finishing my junior year at Westbridge, and by next year there'd be a whole other scandal for kids to be interested in.

Brooke had to know that. She was asking me so she could feel better about herself. If I said no, she shouldn't give up USC, she'd never have to tell Jack and risk his saying that's what she should do. Because it would destroy Brooke if he said that. She'd see it as proof that he did love me more than her.

I looked at Brooke the way I'd looked at Alyssa the other night. Alyssa wasn't just a spoiled selfish kid for me to hate. Brooke wasn't just a golden girl for me to idolize.

They were people. They were my sisters.

"Go to USC," I said.

"Do you mean it?" Brooke asked, and I could see her trying to hide the relief she was feeling.

I glanced at Crystal's pin, remembered the sensation of pricking my finger with it. The pin didn't belong to me. The house didn't belong to me. Even my family—Jack, Brooke, Alyssa—were loaners.

"I mean it," I said.

Brooke ran to where I was sitting and hugged me. I loved her then, for taking the gamble that I might say yes. If I had, I knew she would have gone through with it.

"I'll make it up to you," she said. "I don't know how, but I will."

"It's okay," I said. "Just come to my adoption party. Wherever it is."

Brooke nodded. "I'll be there," she said. "I'll be the happiest person there."

twenty-six

I DREADED GOING BACK to school, but on Monday I had no choice.

I knew what to expect, but I didn't know how it would feel. There are kids in school everyone knows—the popular kids, the star athletes, the high achievers. Everyone knows Brooke, who's all of those things and more.

But I fit in the shadows. Everyone likes me well enough, but no one really thinks about me. I sing in the choir. I try out for school plays, and sometimes I get a small part. I have a solid B average, and a solid B place in school. I'm Willa

Coffey to those kids who know me, and Brooke McDougal's stepsister to everyone who knows her.

But now I was Dwayne Coffey's daughter.

I reminded myself I'd been Dwayne Coffey's daughter back in Pryor, and if I made it through that, I could make it through a school day. But there I'd had Faye to protect me, and Trace, and even Granny Coffey.

With Lauren gone, I only had Brooke. And we didn't have any classes together.

It wasn't like the other kids said anything, at least not to my face. It was more that sense of interrupting conversations you know are about you. My friends were the worst, because they had no idea what to say to me. I could see it in their eyes, hear it in their mumbling words of welcome. They asked if I was okay, but that was where they stopped, as though they didn't know if condolences were in order (my father had died, after all) or if it was better to pretend the past two weeks hadn't happened.

I felt like I was covered in mud and everybody was walking around me very carefully to keep from getting dirty.

Just a couple of boys were deliberately mean to me. I was in the lunch line, and I bumped into Ryan Mitchell, who was standing right ahead of me. He turned to complain and saw who I was.

"It's Killer Coffey," Ryan said. "I'm scared."

Some of the kids laughed.

"Watch out," Kyle Webber said. "She's got a knife." He play-acted cutting Ryan's head off, and the kids laughed even harder.

I didn't know what to do. I couldn't make a joke of it, not after seeing the blood Crystal and my sisters had shed. But I didn't dare start crying, because I was certain if I did, I'd never stop. And I was surrounded by kids in the line, so I couldn't drop the tray and run.

"Leave her alone," Derreck Sanders said. I know Derreck from choir. He has a pitch-pure baritone. He also weighs close to three hundred pounds and plays left tackle. The last I'd heard, he was deciding between Ohio State and Juilliard.

"It was just a joke," Ryan said.

"You're the joke," Derreck said.

I handed my tray to Derreck. "Excuse me," I said, and managed to walk away. I spent the rest of the lunch period in the girls' room, hiding in one of the stalls.

I wasn't hungry anyway.

There was a choir rehearsal after school that day. I thought about skipping it, but if Mom was home when I got there, she'd ask why I wasn't still at school.

Besides, the great thing about choir was I could always

lose myself in it. I was one of many sopranos, a small part of a beautiful whole.

Mrs. Chen saw me when I walked in and asked me how I was doing.

"Fine, thank you," I said, which was what I'd said to all my teachers when they'd asked. It seemed to be what they wanted to hear.

We rehearsed the different songs we'd be singing for the recital, the seniors shining on their solos.

Then we got to "Simple Gifts," and it was my turn to shine. I loved my solo, and it was a big one too: all three stanzas alone, with the choir joining in for the choruses.

I wanted to sing, but I didn't dare. Mrs. Chen had a hard and fast rule that if you missed three practices in a row, you lost your solo. And I'd missed three.

The silence felt so strange, after all the singing. No one picked up on my solo.

"We're waiting for you, Willa," Mrs. Chen said.

"I'm sorry," I said. "I figured you reassigned the solo."

"They wouldn't let me," Mrs. Chen said, gesturing to the choir. "They handed me a petition last practice, insisting you keep it. Everyone in the choir signed it."

"Except me," Derreck said. "My father taught me never to sign anything without a lawyer." He grinned. "I owe you one, Willa."

"Not anymore," I said.

"If you're ready, Willa," Mrs. Chen said.

And I was ready. " 'Tis the gift to be simple, 'tis the gift to be free," I sang, and for the first time in weeks, I knew what I was doing and where I was supposed to be.

twenty-seven

I WAS IN MY ROOM Tuesday night when the phone rang. I was supposed to be catching up on my schoolwork, but I was fantasizing instead. Ever since I'd e-mailed Uncle Martin, I'd been giving a great deal of thought to his cult. I pictured it like a spa, with happy, fulfilled movie stars. Uncle Martin was their resident taxidermist, although I hadn't figured out yet why they would need one.

Everyone was home. Mom was back from her evening class, Alyssa from her tennis practice, Brooke from her orchestra rehearsal. Jack didn't work on Tuesdays.

It was Alyssa who yelled, "Willa, it's for you."

"Who is it?" I yelled back.

"I don't know," she said. "It's some man. He says it's important."

I hoped it was Trace. I hadn't heard from him since I'd left Pryor. I'd given him my cell number, but he could have asked Faye for the home phone.

I went to the den and took the phone from Alyssa. "Willa? This is Sam Whalen, from Pryor."

"Oh, hi, Sam," I said. "Is everything okay?"

"Yes, it is," he said. "But something's come up and I need to talk to you about it."

It's the pin, I thought. *Crystal's family wants the pin back.*

"Okay," I said.

I sensed some hesitation on Sam's part. "You're my client," he said, "but you're also a minor, and what I need to discuss with you is very important. Would you object to putting your mother on the phone?"

It's just a pin, I thought. *And I don't mind giving it back.* "All right," I said. "Should Jack get on too?"

"If you're comfortable with it," Sam said. "It might be better that way."

I gestured to Alyssa and told her to tell Mom and Jack to get on the phone. She ran downstairs, and I could hear them picking up.

"Hi, Sam," Mom said. "Is Faye there?"

"No, she's gone for the day," Sam said. "And as it happens, she doesn't know anything about this. Willa, remember when you were in the office, how we talked about inheritance? How anything Crystal had would pass to Krissi and from Krissi to you?"

"There's nothing to inherit," I said. "I was at the house. There wasn't anything there."

"I'm sorry, Mr. Whalen," Jack said. "But there's no way Willa can accept any inheritance. However small."

"Mr. McDougal, that's not for you to decide," Sam said. "It's Willa's decision to make."

"What am I deciding?" I asked. "The house is a rental. I told Trace he could take Budge's guitar." I remembered the jewelry Trace thought he was slipping past me, but it was hard to believe any of that had value.

"It's not that simple, Willa," Sam said. "I got a phone call yesterday from Mitch Hamlin."

"I remember Mitch," Mom said. "His sister and I were friends."

"Mitch sells insurance now," Sam said. "He got a call from his home office. It seems Crystal had a life insurance policy she bought down in Center City. Her daughters were beneficiaries."

"Her daughters?" Mom asked. "Not Budge?"

"Not Budge," Sam said. "She took out the policy right

after the twins were born. It could be she was afraid of Budge, what he might do to her. We'll never know. But Budge was never arrested for domestic violence, not with her or you or any of his kids, so there was no fraud. It was all perfectly legal, and the insurance company has to pay up. Mitch knew you and Faye were friends, so he guessed I might know who to contact about it."

"How much?" Mom asked.

"Crystal had two hundred and fifty thousand dollar policies for each of her little girls," Sam replied. "Seven hundred and fifty thousand dollars total."

"Seven hundred and fifty thousand dollars?" Mom said. "Willa inherits seven hundred and fifty thousand dollars?"

"That's obscene," Jack said. "Inheriting a fortune because of what Dwayne did. Willa's my daughter, every way but legally, and I can't let her accept money like that."

"Well, there's the rub," Sam said. "Every way but legally, Mr. McDougal. The law says the money is Willa's, so it's up to her to decide."

"What would happen if I refused it?" I asked. "Would Trace get it all?" I imagined him learning he was worth $750,000. That would buy him a lot of guitars and just maybe some peace of mind.

"Most likely he'd end up with nothing," Sam said. "I knew Dwayne wasn't married to Trace's momma, so I played a hunch and spent most of today tracking Mandy Sheldon down. She's living in Reno now. Turns out her parents put a lot of pressure on her to give Trace up for adoption and they instructed her to put 'Father Unknown' on the birth certificate, since they figured it would be easier that way. Only, like a lot of young girls, she took one look at her baby and refused to part with him. Biggest mistake she ever made in her life, she told me, and I gather she's made her share of them."

"But Budge is Trace's father," I said. "Everyone knows that."

"It doesn't matter what everybody knows," Sam said. "In the eyes of the law, you're Krissi's only surviving sibling. You stand to inherit everything."

"Could Trace sue?" Mom asked. "Wouldn't DNA testing prove paternity?"

"I'll tell you the truth, Terri," Sam said. "I've handled a few paternity cases in my day, but this is way past my area of expertise. What I do know is Trace would have to prove he and Krissi had the same father. He can't use any DNA samples from the house, because he's been staying there, so all that DNA is corrupted. Now, Dwayne and Krissi had autopsies, so some hospital has their tissue samples, but I don't know if DNA can be extracted from that. And even if it can be, it's not like Trace can walk into the hospital and demand access. Even if Willa turns the money down, Crystal's folks would most likely not allow Trace anywhere near Krissi's remains."

"They'd get the money?" I asked. "If I turn it down? Trace wouldn't get anything and they'd get it all?"

"Not without a fight," Sam said. "I'm sure there are lawyers who'd take Trace on as a client."

"So when Willa accepts, the money is all hers," Mom said. "She wouldn't have to share it with Trace or Crystal's family."

"Trace might sue and so might Crystal's family," Sam replied. "They might see it the way your husband sees it, that there's something wrong with Dwayne's daughter inheriting like that. And if they do feel that way, they can find a lawyer of their own to tell the courts that Crystal outlived all three of her daughters, which would make them the rightful heirs to the insurance money."

"I thought Krissi was alive when Budge took her," I said. "People saw them together in Ohio."

"It's easy enough to refute eyewitnesses," Sam said. "Autopsy results are tougher, and I hear the autopsy says Krissi died six to twelve hours before she was found in Budge's car. But if it comes to that, the Ballards can hire their own experts to prove otherwise. That's what experts are there for."

"So if Willa accepts the insurance money, she could end

up in court for years," Jack said. "Trace suing her, the Ballards suing her."

"But Willa would win," Mom said. "And even with legal fees, she'd end up with hundreds of thousands of dollars. Isn't that right, Sam?"

"No one can guarantee what juries will do," Sam said. "But Willa certainly has a strong case. And there's always the option of an out-of-court settlement."

"Why should Willa settle?" Mom said. "She's the rightful heir. What happens next? Does the insurance company send her a check or does she have papers to sign?"

"Terri," Jack said. "You can't be serious about this. It's blood money."

"I don't care where the money came from," Mom said. "If Willa's entitled to it, then she should have it."

"I can see you folks have a lot to discuss," Sam said. "Keep in mind, though, this is Willa's decision. Willa, call me if you have any questions, or if you just want to talk."

"Thank you, Sam," I said. Or at least I think that's what I said. Because nothing felt real anymore, except the disgust in Jack's voice and the ecstasy in Mom's.

twenty-eight

"THAT CHANGES EVERYTHING," Mom said.

"What changes everything?" Alyssa asked. "What's going on?"

We were all in the den. Everyone had gravitated upstairs, to me, to the money. The den wasn't built for five people, and I couldn't remember a time when the five of us had been there at the same time.

"Nothing is changed," Jack said. "Willa can't possibly accept the money. You must see that, Terri. How morally wrong it would be."

"Morals have nothing to do with it," Mom said. "Money

doesn't have morals. It's what you do with money that matters. And you can't tell me Willa would do something morally wrong."

"What money?" Brooke asked. "There's an inheritance?"

"Crystal had a life insurance policy," I said. "Her daughters were the beneficiaries, but since they're dead too, the money goes to me. Or maybe me and Trace. Or maybe Crystal's family. Or maybe lawyers if we all sue each other."

"How much money?" Alyssa asked. "Will you be rich, Willa?"

"I don't know," I said. "I guess. There's a quarter of a million for each girl."

"Seven hundred and fifty thousand dollars?" Brooke asked. "Willa, you *are* rich."

"What are you going to buy?" Alyssa asked.

"Girls, please," Jack said. "I'm hoping Willa's learned something being part of this family and she'll turn the money down."

"Learned something?" Mom said. "You'd better believe Willa's learned something."

"Mom," I said. "Jack didn't mean anything—"

"Oh, no," she said. "We all know exactly what he means. He means it's fine for his daughters to have all the advantages money can give you. Private schools, dressage lessons, trips to Europe. But my daughter has to leave her home senior year, work her way through college, because Jack wants her to stay morally pure."

"We didn't ask for those things, Terri," Brooke said. "Mom gave them to us."

"Isn't that nice," Mom said. "You don't even have to ask. How thoughtful of Val to anticipate your every need."

"Terri," Jack said. "We don't talk about Val. Not in front of the girls."

"There's a lot we don't talk about, isn't there, Jack?" Mom said. "Because if we did talk about it, we'd have to see what we've done to Willa, expecting her not to talk about it either."

I looked at Mom, then at Jack. I'd seen her that angry before but I'd never seen Jack look that upset, that close to rage.

It was all about me, I knew. And there was nothing I could do to make things right again. I'd lose Jack if I accepted the money, Mom if I turned it down.

Brooke must have sensed my desperation. "I don't know if this will help," she said. "But I told Willa I'd take the North Carolina scholarship if she wants. That way you could afford to live here, at least until Willa graduates. And she could turn down the insurance money."

"Willa isn't turning down the money," Mom said. "If you loved her, if any of you loved her, you'd be rejoicing for her."

"We love her," Alyssa said, and she looked close to tears. "We love Willa and you, Terri."

"Terri knows that," Jack said. "And she knows taking the money could destroy Willa. It could destroy this family."

"What family?" Mom shouted. "Brooke? Alyssa? They can't wait to move out. You? You deserted us, Jack. You left us in a motel while Budge was on the loose. Me? I've never put Willa first. I've done what you wanted, what was best for your daughters. You call that a family? You call us a family?"

"We *are* a family," Brooke said, her voice quivering. "Willa's my sister, no matter what."

Mom didn't seem to hear her. "You remember Saturdays?" she asked Jack. "When the girls were little? You were always working, so it was up to me to get Alyssa to the club and Brooke to the riding academy. You know what Willa and I used to do? Sit in the car and wait. When Willa asked why she couldn't ride or play tennis, I'd have to explain how we didn't have the money, but wasn't it nice for the two of us to have some time together. Finally, I had the bright idea to ask you to take Willa with you to the ball games. You said yes, and Willa loved it. I've never seen her so happy. She was so happy that Brooke got jealous, so you took both of them with you. That was fine too. Willa loved spending time with Brooke. Do you remember all that, Jack? Is that part of your happy family memory?"

"Terri," Jack said. "Stop, please."

"You don't want to remember this part, do you, Jack?" Mom said. "How Brooke got so jealous, she complained to Val. And Val told you if you didn't spend time alone with your daughters, she'd go to court and petition for sole custody. So you stopped taking Willa. You remember what Val did next? She bought Brooke a horse. A horse! Brooke went back to the riding academy and Willa went back to sitting in the car."

"Mom wanted sole custody?" Alyssa asked. "She didn't want us to see Daddy?"

"She didn't want custody," Brooke said. "She just wanted us to hate Dad like she does."

"Brooke, that's not true," Jack said.

"Don't tell me what's true and what isn't," Brooke said. "You weren't there every night. You know what she'd tell me? That you couldn't be trusted. You'd cheated on her the entire time you were married. And you'd cheat on Terri someday, and she'd leave you too. I shouldn't love her or Willa, because they'd be out of my life soon enough."

"You cheated on Mom?" Alyssa asked. "With Terri?"

"No, not Terri," Jack said. "Terri and I didn't meet until after your mother and I were divorced."

"With some other woman, then?" Alyssa said. "Cheated means affair, right? You had an affair?"

"Lyssie, sweetheart, you're too young to understand," Jack said. "Brooke, I'm sorry. I had no idea your mother was feeding you that kind of poison."

"How could it be poison?" Alyssa asked. "If it was true?"

"Alyssa, please," Jack said. "Brooke, your mother and I, well, we were both young and we made a lot of mistakes. I don't know if I can explain."

"I wish you'd try, Dad," Brooke said. "I've been waiting for that explanation all my life."

"Fine," Mom said. "You explain yourself to your daughters, Jack. Because I'm sick of hearing you explain things. I'm sick of all of you. Willa, darling, I'm sorry. I'm sorry about everything. But I can't stay here. Not now. I've got to get out."

"Mom," I said, but she gestured to me to stay where I was. We watched as she stormed out of the den, heard her rush down the stairs and slam the front door.

"She's coming back, isn't she?" Alyssa asked.

"Of course she is," Jack said. "She's upset, that's all. It'll be all right, Lyssie. I promise you it will."

Promise it to me, I thought, but Jack didn't. No matter how hard I willed him to, he didn't.

twenty-nine

ALYSSA RAN TO OUR ROOM. Jack followed her, but she wouldn't talk to him. Brooke went in, and after a while she came out and told me to sleep in her room, and she'd sleep in mine.

Jack went downstairs. I could hear him on the phone, trying to track Mom down. It only took a couple of phone calls before he found her at Curt and Pauline's. I don't know what he said, but Mom came home around eleven thirty. She and Jack went to their room, and I could hear them talking softly for a long time after that.

I knew I'd never be able to sleep in Brooke's room. I

grabbed a pillow and some blankets from the linen closet and stretched out on the sofa in the den.

I closed my eyes, but my mind was flooded with thoughts. Eventually, I quit even pretending I might sleep. Desperate for anything that might keep me from the basement, from the only comfort I could imagine, I turned the computer on.

There was a reply to the e-mail I'd sent Uncle Martin.

My dear niece Willa,

I'm very glad to hear from you. I've thought about you and Terri Doreen often.

As you may know, God has blessed me with eight daughters. Seven of them have followed the path of righteousness, and live near their mother and me with their husbands and children.

One daughter, however, rejected our world. Rebekah went to the city, where she led a life of sin and degradation. She was dead to me. Then I learned she was ill. She was alone and had no money. My wife begged me to go to the city and do what I could for her. In spite of my grave misgivings, I went.

God, in His infinite mercy, opened my heart to my daughter, and through prayers, her life and her soul were saved. Although she continues to live in the city, she has renounced her old ways and works in a mission house.

After reading your e-mail, I learned what Dwayne has done. It could have been you, your mother, victims of his madness. I could have lost the sister I once loved so dearly, the niece I've never known.

But God has spared you and offered me a second chance. It would mean everything to me if you and Terri Doreen could visit. For such an occasion, Rebekah would certainly come home, and my family would be complete.

With Christ's Word To Guide Us,
Your Uncle Martin Penders

I printed the e-mail, thinking I would show it to Mom the next morning. After what we'd been through, I was sure she'd be glad to hear from Martin. And I knew I wanted to visit him, to meet my cousins, to gain that part of my family, my life, that I'd never had before.

But then I thought about how much a trip to Idaho would cost. We couldn't possibly afford it.

I began shaking with anger. Brooke and Alyssa visited Val's parents three or four times a year. They flew to Orlando for long weekends, spent vacations in Switzerland, France,

China. Alyssa traveled all over the country for tennis tournaments, Brooke for dressage tests.

But Mom and I couldn't afford to go to Idaho to see the only family we had. Our blood family.

I could afford it. I could have enough money to buy anything I wanted. I could have more money than Brooke or Alyssa.

All I had to do was say yes to Sam, to turn my back on Trace, to ignore Crystal's family and their suffering. All I had to do was go against Jack's wishes, something I had never done, something I'd always been too afraid to even think of doing.

I felt as though I would explode if I stayed in the den. I had to go to the one place I felt safe in, my haven, my home. My blood called me.

I opened the door to the hallway. I heard nothing.

Walking as quietly as I could, making sure that no one heard me, I made my way to the basement.

thirty

EVERYTHING WAS THERE as I'd left it: bandages, peroxide, blades.

I took a razorblade out of its cardboard packaging, rubbed my forefinger against its cold, welcoming steel.

How many times had I come down here? How many times had I cut? I did it only when the pressure was so intense, I could think of no other way to release it. I cut to feel pain, because it was safer to feel pain than anger or fear.

I shook with laughter. I'd never known anger or fear before, not this kind. No little slice here, little jab there, could overcome these emotions.

I looked at the blade. It would be so easy, I thought, to cut horizontally, deep into an artery, let my blood flow away, taking my life along with it. So easy.

I was two stories away from everyone. Even if I cried out from the wound, no one would hear me. They never did. If they needed to, they could pretend to themselves it was an accident. Brooke and Alyssa knew I cut, and my body had its share of fading scars. Eventually they'd believe it.

I pressed the blade against my neck. *No tears,* I thought. Not for my sisters, not for me. I hadn't cried since the funeral. No anger, no fear. Some pain, but I was no stranger to pain. Then I would never have to feel anymore.

Mom would get the money. It would pass from Crystal to Krissi, from Krissi to me, from me to Mom. She would never keep it, though. Jack wouldn't let her, and she wouldn't want it. Maybe she'd give it to Trace, the way I'd thought of doing. Let him buy the drugs he used like I used blades.

Budge had five children, I thought. One way or another, he'd found the means to kill us all.

I pictured him then, not the Budge I barely remembered or even the Budge whose picture had been shown endlessly on TV. More a sense of Budge than the man himself. A tired man, drinking again, aware that Crystal feared him, suspecting that she was dreaming of escaping as Terri Doreen had escaped. Wanting nothing more than to sleep away his exhaustion, only to find Kadi in his bed, embraced by Crystal like a babe in the womb.

Where did he keep his hunting knives? In the bedroom, or on the top shelf of a kitchen cabinet? Somewhere he could get to them easily enough but the girls couldn't. Knives like Budge owned were too dangerous for little girls.

He took his favorite, savoring the sharpness of its blade as I savored the sharpness of mine. He intended no harm, I thought. Crystal had felt his blows often enough and that kept her in line. The knife was to frighten her, to impress upon her that it was his bed, not his daughter's.

He carried the knife into his bedroom.

How did he wake them? Did he scream at Crystal, or did he whisper? Maybe he shook her awake, or maybe the sound of his footsteps was enough. If she lived in fear, she'd be able to sense Budge even as she slept.

She pressed her body against Kadi's. If Budge began to beat her, Kadi would escape unscathed. That was probably the best Crystal could hope for, that her babies stay unhurt.

Something about the gesture enraged Budge. Or maybe he was looking for an excuse to start slashing.

There was blood everywhere. Budge was used to blood, to death. He'd killed animals most of his life with his knives. But they'd been clean kills.

This was different—wilder, more exciting.

Kelli Marie screamed.

He heard her running to the bathroom, slamming the door. There was no lock, or if there was, she didn't know how to use it.

Budge raced after her. She hid in the bathtub, behind the shower curtain, as though that would provide her with a cloak of invisibility.

"Come out, sweetie," he said, but she curled her body into a little ball.

"Itsy-bitsy spider," he crooned, "climbed up the water spout."

"Go away, Daddy!" she cried. "I hate you!"

Her fear enraged him. She should know better than to speak to him like that. He'd never hurt her in anger, only when she deserved it. But she was just like her bitch momma—no love, no respect.

No life.

There was blood everywhere. He couldn't clean himself in the bathroom sink, not with Kelli Marie's reproachful eyes staring at him.

He stumbled into the kitchen. Crystal had left a sinkful of dishes. *Just like her,* he thought with comforting resentment. Expecting him to clean up after her and the girls. She didn't care that he worked his butt off at the tannery. The girls were just as bad, never putting their toys away.

He washed himself as best he could. He was damned if he was going to do the dishes.

"Daddy? I had a bad dream, Daddy."

He bent over and picked up little Krissi. She was the youngest of the five children he'd fathered, and the sweetest. No one could accuse him of playing favorites, but if he had one, it would be this little angel.

"You know what chases bad dreams away?" he asked her. "A trip to Dairy Queen. Just the two of us. What do you think about that?"

"Really?" Krissi squealed. "Now?"

"Right now," he said, turning the water off and wiping his hands on the filthy dishtowel. "Let's go to your room and dress you in your best Dairy Queen outfit."

He made sure to carry Krissi, keeping her from seeing things not fit for a baby to see. The two of them selected an outfit and he dressed her quickly, then carried her to the car and placed her in the back seat.

"We're going to a very special Dairy Queen," he said. "One far away from here."

"I love you, Daddy," Krissi said.

He bent down so she could kiss him.

"Go back to sleep, angel," he said. "I'll wake you when we get there."

He began to drive. Almost to his surprise, he found himself going northeast on 54.

He came up with a plan, the best one he could, given the mess he found himself in. He'd leave Krissi with Terri Doreen. She'd taken care of Trace when he'd asked her to. She'd give Krissi a home, and he'd find a place far away from Pryor, from the tannery, from the people who'd held him down all his life.

At first he stopped whenever Krissi asked, but after being in the car for a day or longer, she grew more and more difficult.

Where was Mommy? Where were Kelli Marie and Kadi? She wanted to go home. She was hungry. She was thirsty. She had to potty. Why? Why? Why?

It broke his heart to hear her so unhappy. He told her Mommy and her sisters were in heaven now with Jesus.

"I want Mommy!" she screamed. "I want to go to heaven!"

He was glad he'd brought his knife with him. He kissed his little angel, then gave her the peace she'd begged for. It was a clean kill, one of his best. She felt no pain, just the joy of knowing she'd be united with her momma, her sisters, and Jesus in heaven.

He was the one who suffered, knowing he'd never see

any of them again. He prayed that they could find it in their hearts to forgive him.

He kept driving. He couldn't take Krissi back. It was too far, and he'd run out of cash for the gas he'd need. He'd leave her with Terri Doreen. Somehow she'd find a way to bring Krissi back home, to be with Crystal, Kelli Marie, and Kadi.

It didn't matter what happened to him. He was a dead man. Satan owned his soul and would be coming around to collect it soon enough.

He stopped once to find a phone book, a second time to get directions. Little Krissi wore her blanket shroud, and no one seemed to notice.

He parked the car, impressed by the neighborhood, by how far Terri Doreen had come. If he thought of me at all it was to marvel at the wealth I'd grown up with.

But he probably didn't think of me. He thought of Krissi, her head severed from her body. He couldn't carry her that way. But Terri Doreen had to know who the child was.

He cradled his baby's head in his arms and walked toward the house.

The cops surprised him. He knew they'd be looking for him in Pryor, but he didn't think anyone would care so far away from home. Startled, he dropped Krissi's head and then, enraged that the cop made him commit such a sacrilege, he began swinging wildly. He felt flesh against knife, and then the bitter cold taste of fear. Then he felt nothing.

I knew all this as though I'd been there. I knew it because I was Budge's daughter. His blood coursed through me.

But I wasn't Budge. I could look in a mirror and see his face reflected back at me, but that didn't make me him. I might know his feelings, but that didn't mean they were mine. He was part of my being, but so was Mom. So were Jack and Brooke and Alyssa. So were Granny Coffey and Trace and Mrs. Chen and Curt and Pauline and Derreck and a hundred other people whose lives had been entwined with mine.

I took the peroxide, the bandages, the razorblades. The peroxide and bandages could be returned to the bathroom, hidden in plain sight. The other times I'd made the grand gesture as proof I'd never cut again, I'd buried the razorblades in the garbage, covering them with vegetable peels or eggshells.

This time, though, I held on to the blades. They were as much a part of me as Mom, Jack, my sisters, my brother, Budge.

The blades weren't going to kill me. Budge had five children, and this one, at least, was determined to stay alive.

thirty-one

THE HABITS OF HAPPY families die hard.

It was Wednesday night, and on Wednesdays we always had dinner together. It didn't matter that Mom had poured out years of resentment, that Brooke longed to escape, that Alyssa had learned of Jack's imperfections.

It didn't matter that these four people, whose love had been the one thing I'd been sure of, were strangers to me.

Usually Jack went to great effort with Wednesday supper. But tonight, supper was supermarket roasted chicken, supermarket coleslaw, supermarket pasta salad.

I'd gotten home only a few minutes before supper. There

was a choir practice, and I'd stayed on afterward to talk with Mrs. Chen. After that, I'd called Sam. I'd been in no hurry to get home.

But it was Wednesday, and on Wednesdays, happy families ate together.

We could have been five people eating alone. We could have been five acquaintances, thrown by circumstance into sharing a meal. A couple of times Mom tried to start a conversation. First she asked Brooke, then Alyssa how their day had been.

"Okay," Brooke said.

"I don't want to talk about it," Alyssa said.

Jack looked at me. "How was your day, Willa?" he asked.

I hated what I was going to do, terrified of what would happen. But nothing could be worse than last night.

"I called Sam," I said. "I told him I was taking the money."

Everyone stared at me.

"I told him one third should go to Trace and one third to Crystal's family," I said. "He'll call them for me."

"Willa, you know I think this is wrong," Jack said. "You're doing it anyway?"

I nodded. "I have something to show you." I took the razorblade, nestled in its package, out of my pocket, put it on the table, and pushed it toward him.

I could see the confusion in his eyes.

"This razorblade is my friend, my family," I said. "It's what I turn to when I'm scared you won't love me anymore."

Mom turned pale. "Willa?"

"I cut, Mom," I said. "I have for a long time now. I don't want to anymore, but I don't think I can stop on my own."

"Willa, we would have helped you," Jack said. "You just had to ask."

"I couldn't ask!" I cried. "I cut because I couldn't ask. I couldn't ask for anything. I couldn't ask to finish high school here. I couldn't ask for voice lessons. I couldn't ask for anything that costs money because I'm not supposed to notice that Brooke and Alyssa get whatever they want. So I cut. And Jack, it helped. It got me through a lot of bad moments. It scares me to think what things would have been like if I didn't cut, but the cutting scares me more now. So I'm taking the money. I'm going to pay for the mortgage, so I don't have to be yanked from school in the middle of senior year. I'm going to pay for voice lessons, because singing means more to me than almost anything else in life. I'm going to pay for college for me and for Mom. I'm going to pay for therapy, so I won't need razorblades anymore. I love you, Jack. I know you say you love me. But I can't keep on like this anymore. I won't. I'm taking the money."

"Did you know?" Jack asked, looking at his daughters. "Did either of you know Willa was hurting herself?"

"They didn't know anything," I said. "That's why I cut. So no one would know anything."

We all heard my cell ring. "I'm taking it," I said, even though there was a rule that we never left supper for a phone call. I walked out of the dining room so I could talk in private.

"Willa? It's Trace."

"Yes," I said. "I know."

"I spoke to that lawyer of yours," he said. "I guess you told him to?"

"I called him this afternoon," I said.

"I didn't know if I should thank you or sue you," Trace said. "He said I could do one or the other, but not both."

"Have you decided?" I asked. "I mean, about suing me."

"Well, the way I see it, the law's never been on my side," Trace said. "Besides, I've gone through every inch of this house, and the only thing I found was twelve bucks and forty-one cents in Kelli Marie's piggy bank. I was going to split it with you."

"You can have it all," I said.

"Don't mind if I do," Trace said. "Look, there's another reason I called. The rent's coming due here in a few days, and I don't see much point sticking around. I got Budge's guitar.

I got the twelve bucks. I guess I'll be taking off for Nashville next week."

"You'll stay in touch, won't you?" I asked. "I don't want to lose you, Trace."

"I don't get lost that easy," Trace said. "I'm a bad penny. I always turn up. Anyway, they sent Budge's ashes back home, and Granny Coffey's threatening to throw them in the trash. I thought maybe we should bury them or something. Have a little service. Not like Crystal and the girls. I don't know any church would have him."

"We could scatter his ashes," I said. "If you know someplace he might like."

"He loved the woods," Trace said. "I think you should come down, Willa. I know you don't remember him, and he was an evil sonavabitch, but he was our daddy, and it's right for us to be there."

I felt myself back in the basement, holding on to the razorblade, feeling Budge's rage, his insanity. I needed to see him blow away. "Yes," I said. "I'll be there."

"Good," Trace said. "Give us a chance to say goodbye. And Willa . . ."

"Yes?" I said.

"Thank you."

I walked back to the dining room, feeling everyone's eyes on me.

"That was Trace," I said. "He has Budge's ashes. We're going to scatter them in the woods. I'll fly down on Friday. Sam said he could give me a small advance on the money if I needed it."

"There's no talking you out of it?" Jack asked. "Accepting the insurance?"

I shook my head. "I'm sorry," I said. "I'll understand if you don't want to be my father anymore."

"No," Jack said. "Of course I'm your father. I'll always be your father. If you doubt that, Willa, then I really have failed you. I'm sorry." He paused for a moment, then turned to Mom. "We have to go with her," he said. "Back to Pryor. You know that, don't you, Terri? We've asked Willa to do too much alone as it is."

"I don't know," Mom said. "It scares me to go back. It scares me to think about Budge, my time with him."

"It scares me too, Mom," I said. "But he was my father, and I've got to see this through."

"I want to go too," Alyssa said.

We stared at her.

"No, I mean it," she said. "Daddy's always talking about us being a family. Well, families do stuff together. Like go to funerals."

"You have your tournament," I said. "I'd never ask you to give that up."

"You didn't," Alyssa said. "This was my idea. I'm going with you."

"I'll go also," Brooke said. "What's another dressage test in my life? You're my sister. This is a lot more important."

"You can't just change your plans like this," Mom said. "Your grandparents are flying in. Your mother expects to see you in Brussels."

Brooke looked thoughtful. "The service will be Saturday," she said. "Grandy and Gram can fly in to Dallas. We'll meet them there Sunday and fly to Brussels from there. You'll be tired, Lyss, for the first day of play, but you'll get there on time."

"Willa can come too," Alyssa said, turning to me. "You can afford it now. Fly to Brussels with us, and then go to Madrid to see Lauren, and come back in time for the quarterfinals. I'll still be playing, I promise."

For a moment, I was tempted. I would have loved to see Lauren, and now I was sure she'd be glad to see me. This was exactly the sort of trip I'd seen Brooke and Alyssa take whenever they wanted. And Alyssa was right. For the first time in my life, I had the money to indulge myself.

I'm not sure whether it was remembering what Pastor Hendrick had said about temptations, or sensing what Jack must be thinking, or simply reminding myself where the money had come from. Maybe it was all of that.

"I don't think so," I said to Alyssa with a smile. "It sounds like a lot of money, but there's an awful lot I need to do with it. Besides, I'd rather save up and see you at Wimbledon."

"Then it's settled," Brooke said. "I'll call Gram right now and tell her. Then I'll make the plane reservations. Terri? You *are* coming with us, aren't you?"

"Mom?" I said. "Not for Budge. For me."

Mom took a deep breath. "For you," she said. "For me. For all of us."

thirty-two

IT WAS A DAMP GRAY DAY, but there was a gentle spring breeze that spoke of better times.

After breakfast, Mom, Jack, and I had gone to the Penderses' gravesite. Curt and Pauline had sent a dozen white tulips, and I put one on each of the brothers and sisters Mom had never known, and one for her mother and father.

Then I read Mom the e-mail I'd gotten from Martin. And for Mom and me, one last piece of our missing family was restored.

Faye had taken Brooke and Alyssa to the spot in the

woods Trace had selected. Mom knew exactly where it was, and we had no trouble finding them.

Trace was already there, with Granny Coffey. Sam had come also. And so had Pastor Hendrick.

"It's good of you to be here," Jack said to him.

"He was a member of my flock," Pastor Hendrick replied. "And he's in my prayers."

"I can't forgive him," Mom said. "I'll never be able to."

"No one expects you to," Pastor Hendrick said. "But for all his evil, Dwayne is Willa's father, and Trace's and Kelli Marie's and Kadi's and Krissi's. There must have been some good in him to father such beautiful children."

"His momma was trash," Granny Coffey said. "And his daddy was weak. Budge was trouble from the day he was born till the day he died. Never thought I'd outlive him, though. I buried my only son, and three of my great-grandbabies, and now this." She spat contemptuously. "Well, get on with it," she said. "Dust to dust. Ashes to ashes. This was your idea, boy. No point dawdling."

"I think we should have some kind of prayer," Trace said. "I know the Lord's Prayer. Maybe we should say that."

Pastor Hendrick began the prayer and we all joined in. In the distance a deer paused, then, seeing us, ran on.

Trace opened the box and scattered the ashes onto the forest floor. "I love you, Daddy," he said.

Those were words I could barely remember saying, would never say again. Like Mom, I didn't know that I'd ever forgive him.

Still, I placed the white tulips over Budge's ashes. Then, surrounded by my family, my friends, and with the sweet cry of meadowlarks as a choir, I gave the gift of song to my fathers.